FAMILY MATTERS

Tamara Merrill

AUGUSTUS FAMILY TRILOGY
BOOK TWO

This book is a work of fiction. Names, characters, businesses, organizations, places, events, and incidents are either the product of the author's imagination or are used fictitiously. Any resemblance to actual persons, living or dead, events, or locales is entirely coincidental.

To Theresa, Who said I could.

Other Books by Tamara Merrill

Family Lies, Augustus Family Trilogy, Book 1

Table of Contents

The City Chronicle
September 30, 1944

Tattletales by Sharon Chatsworth

Despite the continuing ill health of their patriarch, Walter Augustus, this reporter is delighted to report that our fair city's Augustus family will soon have reason to rejoice. I have it from a very good source that Minette Rothchild Augustus, whose whereabouts have been unknown by this reporter for more than five years, has arrived in England. While her stories of wartime in France will be interesting, I, for one, am much more interested in where Sylvia (Mrs. John) Augustus has been keeping herself these many months and what, exactly, she has been doing.

Chapter One

After the Allied invasion of Normandy in June 1944, Minette began to believe that the Allies would soon liberate France, and she allowed herself to look forward to reuniting with her son and his family. She was dismayed when she realized that almost five years had passed without any contact with John or the Augustus family. It wasn't that she hadn't thought about them or worried about them, but she'd known that if she tried to contact them, it would be dangerous for her fellow Resistance workers, and so she had allowed the months to slip past.

Now, with the Allies in the war, and even as the French Resistance movement increased its activity against the Nazis, Minette began to make plans to leave France. On August 25, with the city of Paris safely in the hands of the Allied troops, she knew it was time to put aside her work with the Resistance and return to life with her son and grandson.

The mail was still confused and the phone service was minimal at best, so she didn't worry when she found it impossible to reach

John in England and let him know of her plans. They would see each other soon. As she crossed the channel, her heart lifted, and Minette allowed herself to rejoice in the work the Resistance had done and what they had accomplished. Too many of her brave friends were dead, captured, missing, or injured, but they had made a difference, a very real difference, and now it was time to return to her family in the States. She looked back at the receding French coastline and wondered when, if ever, she would return to her homeland.

Minette arrived in England with little more than the clothes on her back and a few francs in her pocket. There were no cabs at the dock, so she shouldered her duffle and walked to the AmCo office. All around her the bombing had smashed the buildings, but in the distance she could see the dome of St. Paul's Cathedral, and the people she passed smiled and nodded and appeared to be going about the everyday business of life. Each and every person she passed seemed to have taken Winston Churchill's admonition, "Never give in, never, never, never, never—in nothing, great or small, large or petty—never give in," to heart.

Arriving at the office building, she was relieved to find that, despite some damage, the building was inhabited and the AmCo office was open. Her first indication that something wasn't right came when the young woman at the desk, who had greeted her politely, became visibly flustered when Minette asked to see John Augustus.

"Who may I say is asking, madam?" she managed to stammer. But when Minette stated her name and her desire to surprise her son, the poor girl paled and rose from the desk. "Please make yourself comfortable." She gestured toward the chairs. "I'll be right back." And she fled down the hall.

Minette stilled and for a moment she felt fear, but she pushed it aside. Obviously, John was not expecting her; perhaps his staff believed that she was lost to the cause or had even been killed. Although, she admitted to herself, it didn't seem like John to have spoken about her work in the Resistance. She smiled slightly and imagined how happy John would be to see her alive and well and ready to return home.

Her smile faltered as the receptionist returned followed by a young man she'd never met. "Mrs. Augustus"—he held out his hand in greeting—"I'm Stephen Alistair. Please step into my office and we can talk."

She followed him, refused his polite offer of tea, and braced herself for whatever he had to say. Even with the ability to conceal her emotions that she had developed over the war years, Minette's felt her heart pound and the color drained from her face as she learned that

John had been missing since January 1941. "That's almost four years," she managed. "Hasn't he contacted anyone?"

"Not that I am aware of, madam. I've asked Kristina to place a call to the States and, as soon as she gets Sam on the line, she'll let us know. I'm sure he can explain everything to you."

Minette clutched her hands in her lap and took a deep breath. Unable to speak, she nodded slightly. Fear took her breath away and she began to tremble.

On the other side of the Atlantic, Sam was just leaving for his office when Chris called from the doorway. "Dad, you've got a phone call. Mom says it's important."

Sam smiled at his gangly, seventeen-year-old son and his newly deep voice, tossed his briefcase into the car, and hurried back to the house. One look at Helen's face and he knew that something important was happening. "It's Minette," she said and handed him the phone.

"Minette?" He brought the phone to his ear and said again, "Minette? Is it really you? Are you okay? Where are you?"

Minette's rich voice and charming accent floated out of the receiver. "I'm fine, Sam. I'm in London, and they are telling me that no one knows where John is living—that he's been missing a long time."

"Not exactly missing. He's joined the RAF. I'm surprised he didn't tell you."

"He had no way to reach me." Minette's voice broke. "What happened? Tell me quickly."

"In October 1940, the house where he was living with Valerie was destroyed in the Blitz. John and Michael survived, but Valerie was killed." Sam took a deep breath and continued speaking into Minette's silence. "He took it very hard. At first, he didn't return our calls, and when I finally was able to speak to him, he asked to be left alone to handle it in his own way. The office was shut down through the holidays, and we all assumed that he'd be back at work in January, but instead he sent a telegram saying he'd joined the RAF."

"And Michael, where is he?"

"He's in London with Annie. We don't have an address and have been unable to locate them, but John assured us that all was well."

"Sam, all is not well. My son and my grandson have been allowed to disappear."

"John is an adult, Minette. He makes his own decisions."

"Perhaps, but we are family. And family does not allow family to disappear."

Sam wanted to protest. After all, Minette had been out of touch with the family even longer than John, but a wave of guilt overwhelmed him and instead he said, "John hasn't disappeared, Minette. He's serving in the military, in a war. And I'm sure he knows that we are taking care of things at home. AmCo is producing supplies for the military at a greater rate than ever, supplies that all the Allied troops need."

"Taking care of business perhaps, but you are not taking care of Michael and John, or even Annie."

"I tried to find them, Minette. No one in London could tell me anything. The staff was unaware that Valerie was living with John or that she was pregnant." Minette caught her breath on the word *pregnant*, but Sam hurried on. "John had somehow managed to keep his private life a secret. The staff didn't even know that Michael and Annie were in London. The landlord and the few neighbors I located spoke highly of Valerie and of what a lovely couple they were and how sad it was that she and her unborn child had been killed in the bombing. No one seemed to know them well, but everyone seemed to feel that it was natural that John would be laid low by his grief, and they weren't surprised that he'd gone away with his son and the nanny. No one could tell me where they might be. In fact, the general agreement seemed to be that he had returned to the States. When we finally heard that he'd joined the RAF, we decided to leave him alone. He seemed to be doing what he needed to do, following in your footsteps and giving his all for the war effort in order to heal himself. I can tell you that he has not been killed in action, and I'm sure that Michael is being well cared for by Annie."

"What about Sylvia? Has she heard from John? Hasn't she tried to find Michael?"

Sam paused and took a deep breath. "A lot has happened since you moved to France, Minette. Too much to explain in one phone call, but Sylvia is not able to search for Michael, and I'm sure she hasn't had any contact with John."

"But she's his mother. Surely, she must be worried."

"Sylvia was hospitalized about four years ago, and she has not asked about either Michael or John in all that time. In fact, the doctor has felt it best that they are never mentioned to her."

The line hummed as Minette digested this. In her silence, Sam could feel her shock and decided not to add any details of Sylvia's treatment until Minette was back in the States. After a long pause, Minette said carefully, "I'll find them, Sam. I'll find them and bring them home."

"Tell me what I can do to help."

"Right now, I need money and a place to stay."

"That's no problem. Stephen will take care of everything you need and he'll help arrange transportation back to the States when you are ready."

"Thank you, Sam. I'll keep you informed, but I won't be back until I find my family."

There were shortages in London but Minette reveled in the hot water and scented soap provided by the hotel where Stephen had found her a room. The long, hot bath was a luxury she hadn't enjoyed in years, and, as she lay back against the rim, she allowed herself to remember life in the States, life as a member of the wealthy Augustus clan. A life filled with plenty, where there were no hardships and no real problems, as different as possible from the life even the wealthiest people in France had endured during the Occupation. Those days of long ago almost seemed like a story, a fairytale, a dream. Even so, she was glad her mother had journeyed to the States and found her. The time they had been able to spend together in Paris had been so precious and had healed so many wounds. Minette finished her bath and began to create a plan for finding John and Michael. Tomorrow, she'd talk to the neighbors again. Surely someone would remember something.

Early the next morning, Minette asked for directions at the hotel desk and then hailed a cab to take her to John's last-known address. Immediately after giving the cab driver the address, it was apparent that this might not be as easy as she'd believed.

The cabby pushed his hat up and scratched under the brim. "You can't go there, Missus. There aren't any houses anywhere around there. They've all been blown up or torn down."

"All?"

"Yes, ma'am. All. The damn Krauts—pardon my language—have been bombing that area over and over. Everyone has moved away."

"Can you take me close?"

"Certainly, but there isn't much to see."

"That's all right. I just think I need to see it for myself."

She stood on what she thought had been a street corner and gazed about. Blocks and blocks were completely flattened. Most of the rubble had been pushed into piles, but there was no place for anyone to take shelter, much less for a family to live. Tears filled her eyes and she impatiently wiped them away. Tears wouldn't help her find John.

"Where have the people gone?" she asked quietly.

"Wherever they can, ma'am. Some are dead. Some went to family. Lots of the children were sent to the country." Minette nodded slightly and the cabby continued, "Are you looking for someone?"

Minette nodded again and managed to say, "My son and grandson. They lived here and now no one knows where they are."

"There are ways to look, ma'am. The Registry tries to keep track of people, and if the child was sent away, they'll have records of where and when."

"No, they are still here in London somewhere. My son is with the RAF, but his son is living with the nanny."

"I'd start with the RAF office then. They should know where their men are located."

"Excellent!" Minette smiled at the cabby. "That makes sense to me. Do you know how I would do that?"

"If you don't know his squadron, I'd start at Uxbridge. It's not far, and I'm sure they could help you."

In Uxbridge, Minette assaulted the English bureaucracy and after talking to a variety of petty bureaucrats she was able to find that John had indeed joined Eagle Squadron No.71 and records indicated he'd still been with the squadron in September 1942 when the squadron had been transferred to the US Army Air Force, becoming the 334th Fighter Squadron of the 4th Fighter group. Learning that the 334th was based in Essex, her heart lifted. She believed in the Americans' attention to detail and organization, and she was sure that John, as an American serving in an American squadron, would be easy to locate.

Minette returned to her cab with a lighter heart and a determination to proceed immediately to the airbase in Essex. The cabby, who by now was invested in her search, was happy to oblige. As he drove from Uxbridge across London to Essex, he chatted away about the brave young men who flew the airplanes and how sure he was that they could stop the awful Blitz. "I hear they can even find these new V-2 rockets and shoot them out of the sky. The Krauts don't have a chance against our boys!"

But in Essex the news wasn't as good. Minette was informed that John's plane had been shot down over the channel in July and there was no record of his rescue. He was missing in action. Her heart dropped. All the happiness of the last hours drained away. She'd been so sure that John and Michael were somewhere close.

Minette managed to ask why his family had not been notified and was shocked to learn that John had indicated that he had no next of kin on his enlistment papers. "But how can that be?" she stammered.

The young corporal blushed slightly. "It's not that unusual, ma'am. Some men just want to disappear, and a war is a good place to do that."

The City Chronicle
October 10, 1944

Tattletales by Sharon Chatsworth

In a time of war, there are so many sad stories to report and today this reporter learned that John Augustus has been missing in action since July. The family, when contacted, declined to be interviewed, and so I can bring you no details. Perhaps it is true that John is estranged from the family, and one can only suppose that the disappearance of Sylvia is somehow involved. But I, for one, love a good mystery, and you can be sure that the truth will come out.

Chapter Two

Because the Army Air Force was unable to supply any information that would help her locate John, Minette turned to checking the hospitals, reasoning that if he had been rescued, he might be injured, perhaps even unable to speak. She was deeply shaken but sure that John was alive, and so she made her plan and began her search.

Visits to the London hospitals broke her heart. So many civilians wounded by the Blitz, so many soldiers, airmen, and sailors with horrible injuries but brave smiles. She heard tales of the exploits performed by the brave airmen of the 334th, but no one was able to tell her about John.

Having exhausted the London hospitals, she expanded her search, and at last enlisted the services of the cabby, Henry Smyth, who had helped her that first horrible day. They journeyed the 163 kilometers to Birmingham where she'd been told that many wounded were being cared for at the new Queen Elizabeth Hospital.

As they drove, they talked and shared life stories. Minette realized how very kind and caring this man was, and he, in turn, resolved to himself to do whatever he could to help this beautiful woman find her son and grandson.

The hospital was very busy. Local businesses and university buildings had been converted into wards to treat both the civilian and military casualties; some wards that were meant to hold four beds contained sixteen. She was directed to the records department and while her request for information about John resulted in a long search of available records, she was unable to find anything.

She turned away from the information desk and Henry, who had been waiting patiently, took her arm and suggested that they get a cup of tea. Minette nodded and allowed him to guide her to a nearby tearoom where she gratefully sank into a chair and allowed Henry to order.

Minette glanced about and noticed that the room was full of young nurses, ambulatory patients still in their pajamas and robes, and family members of all ages. She noted the terrible injuries and the caring attitude of the staff and family members and the determination of the patients "to get on with it."

She smiled at Henry. "Thank you for your kindness, Henry. I could not have managed this alone."

He started to protest that it was his pleasure when a lovely young nurse jumped from her chair and hurried to their table. "Mrs. Augustus, is it really you? I thought it was, but when I heard you speak, I knew it was. Why are you here? Is Mr. Augustus alright?"

The questions tumbled out so quickly that Minette could only gaze at the nurse unsure of who was asking and how or what to answer.

"It's me, ma'am. Annie."

"Annie!" Minette's limbs unfroze and she jumped to her feet and hugged the young woman close. "Oh, Annie! I'm so happy to see you! But if you're a nurse, where's Michael?"

Annie laughed. "He's with my ma and da on the farm in Wales and happy as a clam last I heard."

"Sit, Annie." Minette tugged her down into a chair. "Tell me everything. Where is John? And why is Michael in Wales and, *Mon Dieu*, just tell me everything."

Annie laughed and composed herself. "Where shall I begin? What do you know?"

"Begin at the beginning, of course. I know nothing, nothing that makes sense."

Annie began the story with Sylvia's accident and hospitalization. She told of her journey to London with Michael, of how delightful the few days with Valerie had been, and then the bombing. "The bombs began raining down, so we went to the shelter. Valerie was in labor and when the all-clear sounded about four o'clock, I went for the midwife. She was busy and couldn't come, but Mr. Augustus came home so that helped.

"When the bombing began again, I took Michael to the shelter, but Valerie wanted to wait for the midwife. By the time the midwife got there, it was too late to move Valerie to the shelter. After the baby was born..." Minette gasped but waved her hand for Annie to continue her story. "So after the baby was born, the midwife sent John to the shelter with the babe and told him to come back to help move Valerie.

"A bomb hit the house directly, and Valerie and the midwife were killed. Mr. Augustus was devastated. He disappeared, and I couldn't find him. I did the best I could, but I had no money and no idea what to do. I had no idea how to take care of a newborn babe."

Minette reached out and held Annie's hand tightly and nodded for her to continue. "We were down in the tube station and this nice man told me they were evacuating the mothers and children to Wales, and since my family is there and I had no more money for food, it seemed like the right thing to do. So I took the children to Wales."

"Oh, Annie. You brave girl! You did exactly the right thing. But the baby? No one knows that the baby was born!"

"Mr. Augustus knows."

"Yes. But we don't know where he is, and he never mentioned the baby to anyone before he joined the RAF."

Henry couldn't contain himself another moment. "Is it a girl or a boy?"

Minette laughed and patted his arm. "Exactly right, Henry. Which is it?"

"She's a lovely girl. Pretty as a picture and smart as a whip. Ma and Da think the world of them both. Michael insisted that her name was Elizabeth, so that's what she was christened, Elizabeth Anne."

"It's a wonderful name"—Henry beamed—"and a wonderful story. I'm sure now that we will find the father, too."

Minette smiled at his exuberance. "Oh, Henry." She laughed and then turned back to Annie. "You are a wonder, Annie. I don't know how to thank you for keeping Mich—" She stopped and corrected herself. "…the children safe. I will go to Wales at once."

Annie nodded. "What about Mr. Augustus, ma'am? Where is he?"

"We don't know," Minette admitted. "His plane was shot down over the channel. I believe he is alive. I'd know if he wasn't, and I won't stop looking until I find him. But now I want to collect the children and get them back to the States."

"I can't go with you, ma'am. I'm on duty, and it will be weeks before I have enough time off to go home."

"I'll go with you, Minette," Henry declared.

"You don't have to do that, Henry," she protested.

"Oh, yes, I do! I've come this far, and now I want to meet these children and help you find John." He grinned at Minette. "I love a good story, and this is better than any book I've ever read."

Armed with Annie's careful instructions, Minette and Henry set out the next morning. They covered the 218 kilometers from Birmingham, England to Port Talbot, Wales in cheerful camaraderie. As they drove, they shared more life stories and Minette learned that Henry had been a college professor before the war. She explained that she'd left America to go to France to care for her mother, but she didn't mention her work with the Resistance and she didn't pry into Henry's reason for driving a cab.

They reached Port Talbot and stopped for a late lunch in a pub where the menu was restricted due to rationing, but the proprietress served them a mouthwatering rabbit stew and thick, rough bread which was so delicious, soaked in the broth, that they didn't notice the lack of butter. Their high spirits attracted attention and as they finished eating, the owner, Mrs. Jones, introduced herself to them and asked why they were in town.

Minette smiled happily. "We've discovered that my grandson is here in Glamorgan, and we've come to take him home to the States. I haven't seen him in over four years."

"A happy ending! Lovely! There are so many children here and so many have no family left to claim them. Who is he biding with?"

"The Bowens. Oliver and Adenydd. They live in the Vale of Glamorgan. Do you know them?"

"I can't say as I do, but the Vale is a good long ways from here and with the blackout it isn't possible to get there at night." Minette's face fell, and Henry reached out and patted her hand. "Don't you worry." Mrs. Jones smiled broadly. "I've got one room empty so you can stay here for the night and be on your way in the morning. You'll be seeing the child by noon."

"But we aren't …" Minette started to protest but was stopped by Henry's warm hand on hers as he assured Mrs. Jones that the room would be fine. Minette looked at him, but he avoided her eyes as they followed Mrs. Jones first to the desk and then to the room above the pub.

When the door closed, Henry grinned at her. "You should've seen your face! Don't worry. I'll behave like a perfect gentleman and sleep on the floor, and we'll be on our way first thing after sunup."

Minette laughed. "I've been in worse situations than this. I know how to take care of myself. And I'm quite sure that your company will make the time go faster." She grinned. "Let's go explore the town before the sun goes down and the lights go off."

Rising early the next morning, they took turns freshening up, had a quick cup of tea and a scone, and then were back in the car and on the road again. They saw only military vehicles, and Henry commented on her luck in having gas coupons from AmCo. "If we had to travel with a horse and cart, I'm not sure when we'd see these grandchildren of yours."

"Grandchildren," Minette murmured. "How strange that there are two. I keep forgetting about the baby." She shook her head sadly. "Not a baby anymore. She'll be almost three and Michael is seven by now. I don't imagine he'll remember me, but I wonder what he knows about his parents, his family."

They fell silent and watched the rugged coastline turn to rich, rolling agricultural land dotted with cows and sheep and an occasional farm.

At last, they reached the lane that would lead to the Bowen farm. Minette sat with her hands clasped tightly in her lap. Henry pulled the car over to the side and stopped. He laid his hand on hers. "All right now," he said. "Are you ready?" Minette nodded slightly. "Take a deep breath then and here we go." He put the car in gear and eased forward.

"I've said it before; you're a kind man, Henry. Thank you."

Around the last bend they saw the house with its thatched roof, white-washed barns and sheds, and the rugged rock garden walls. In the yard, a rotund woman was pegging clothes on the line and two children chased each other and a large dog. The woman turned and dropped the shirt she was holding back into the basket and came toward the car. "You'll be Mrs. Augustus, I expect. Annie sent a telegram last night." She grasped Minette's hand. "I haven't told the children. I wasn't sure what to say."

The children rushed around the side of the house and stopped to stare at the strangers in the yard. Minette smiled at them. "Hello, Michael," she said.

He strode forward, hand extended. "Hello, ma'am."

His accent surprised her. *Of course*, she reminded herself, *he'd have an accent. He's been living here for three years.* She extended her hand and he shook it carefully. "Do you know who I am?" she asked.

He shook his head. "I don't think so. Should I?"

Minette shook her head, slightly unsure how to answer.

"Do you know me?" he asked. She nodded. "And Elizabeth?" She shook her head no.

"Michael." Henry stepped in. "This is your grandmother, come all the way from France to fetch you."

Michael's eyes widened, and he reached for Elizabeth's hand. He didn't say anything but seemed to be studying Minette carefully.

Minette said, "The last time I saw you, you were no bigger than Elizabeth is now. I went away to live in France."

"Do you know my father? And Valerie?"

"Your father is my son. And I know your mother, Sylvia, but I don't know Valerie."

"Valerie says you are telling the truth." Michael nodded. "I remember my mother. She doesn't like me." Minette looked at Mrs. Bowen for guidance. She wanted to protest, but something in the boy's tone stopped her.

Mrs. Bowen shrugged and raised her eyebrows significantly.

"Why are you here?" Michael asked carefully. "Where is my father?"

"I'm here to take you back to the United States to live with our family."

"What about Elizabeth? She's my family."

Minette was astounded by his self-assurance and his protective attitude toward the little girl. She wondered what would be the right thing to say. Elizabeth was John's child, actually more his child than Michael was, and yet how would the rest of the family react to an unknown child arriving in their midst? None of the rest of the Augustus family even knew that Valerie had given birth or that the child had survived. But surely, if John were here, he'd want Elizabeth to be taken care of, despite the gossip it might cause.

"If it is possible, Elizabeth will come to the States with us."

"Elizabeth has to stay with me," Michael said flatly. "She's mine!"

"There now, Michael. Take Elizabeth in and wash up, and we'll have a cup of tea and a bite to eat." As the children headed toward the open kitchen door, Mrs. Bowen dropped her voice and continued, "He's a lovely big brother."

"I can see that. But what does he mean when he says Elizabeth is his?"

Mrs. Bowen hesitated and then decided the truth was best. "Michael believes that he sees Valerie and that he can hear her, that she told him that Elizabeth was his on the night she died." Minette gasped. "Here in Wales," Mrs. Bowen said carefully, "we have no fear of fairies or messages from the dead."

"But—" Minette began to protest.

Mrs. Bowen held up her hand. "Wait. Come in and have tea and get to know the children."

They settled around the large, well-scrubbed kitchen table with cups of tea and thick slices of freshly baked bread spread with both butter and jam. Minette praised the food, and Mrs. Bowen explained that while many things were rationed, they made their own butter, and the jam was from wild berries that grew so sweet that no sugar was needed. The adults talked about the war and conditions in London and assured Mrs. Bowen that Annie had looked well and happy.

Michael studied both Minette and Henry carefully and finally he asked Henry, "Are you my grandfather?"

Henry smiled. "No. I'm a friend of your grandmother's. I'm just along to help her in any way I can."

Michael considered this for a moment and then nodded. "Elizabeth and I are very happy here," he said solemnly. "I think we should wait for our father to come and get us. Right, Lizzy?" Elizabeth nodded and slipped her hand back into his. Obviously, whatever Michael wanted was right.

Mrs. Bowen rose from her chair and stood behind the two children, placing a hand on each shoulder. "It's been lovely having you stay with us but it's time to go home."

"This is home," Michael declared. "My father can find us here."

"Aye, this will always be a home for you and Elizabeth," Mrs. Bowen said kindly, "but it's not your only home. And I promise you your father will find you in the United States, perhaps even find you more quickly there. You need to go with your grandmother."

"And Elizabeth?" Michael asked suspiciously.

"And Elizabeth," Henry declared. "We'll figure it out, lad. Where you go, Elizabeth will go,"

"Cross your heart?"

"Cross my heart," Henry said soberly.

Michael turned to Minette. She smiled. "Cross my heart, Michael."

"When do we have to go with you?"

As Minette started to respond, Mrs. Bowen reached out and touched her hand, smiled at Michael, and then said, "I think you should take Elizabeth outside for a bit and allow your grandmother to finish her tea."

Michael rose obediently and drew Elizabeth away from the table and out the kitchen door.

The door closed and Minette lowered her cup to the saucer. "I don't think Michael wants to go home with me, and I don't know if Elizabeth can travel with us. I don't know the law."

"I think," Henry spoke slowly, "that no one will stop the daughter-in-law of Walter Augustus from taking a war orphan back to the United States." He held up his hand to stop Minette's protest. "I know she is your son's daughter, but it might be best to simply declare that she is an orphan. There will be fewer questions." Mrs. Bowen nodded. "And," Henry continued, "you have to remember that not only is this the only home Michael remembers, he has no idea who we are or what going to the United States means."

"Oh, Henry." Minette frowned slightly. "Of course, you are right." She turned to Mrs. Bowen. "If you don't mind, I'll stay in the village a few days, make the arrangements, and let the children get to know me. Would that be all right?"

"That seems like a fine plan. Oliver and I will talk to Michael and assure that he understands why you are here and that it is a good thing."

"What about the girl?"

"Elizabeth loves Michael as much as Michael loves Elizabeth. As long as they are together she will be happy."

Back in the village they found lodging, and Minette placed a call to Sam. As they waited for the operator to call them back, they sat silent, each wrapped in their own thoughts and memories. At last, the call came through, and Henry turned away to give Minette privacy, but she caught his arm and stayed his departure.

Rapidly, she filled Sam in on the events of the last two days, of finding Annie and Michael, and of the existence of Elizabeth. Sam was astounded, but he immediately agreed that Minette should bring both children home. His legal mind worked quickly, and he asked, "Does she have a baptism certificate?"

"She does," Minette acknowledged, "but it states that both mother and father are unknown. Annie's parents are listed as her godparents. She has no other guardian. Henry thinks it would be possible to bring her with me as a war orphan."

Sam didn't ask who Henry might be, he simply considered the suggestion and said, "Yes, I think that might work, the guardians will be able to sign for you to take her out of Wales. How long will it take for you to get back to London?"

"We can leave in a day or two. I'd say we need a week."

"I'll take care of the paperwork and have Stephen find you transportation. And Minette…" Sam hesitated a moment. "It would be best if you don't mention to anyone that John is the child's father."

Minette nodded even though Sam couldn't see her. "Yes, I understand."

The Bowens were able to reassure Michael that he and Elizabeth should go with his grandmother to the United States, and Henry was able to convince him that the journey would be a wonderful adventure, that Elizabeth would be safe, and that they would, indeed, like his cousins who lived there. Henry drove the 218 kilometers back to London, stopping only for food and necessary breaks. Michael entertained Elizabeth by pointing out birds, animals, and clouds until she fell asleep, and then he turned his attention toward Minette.

"Grandmother," he began politely, "is my father fighting the war?"

"He is."

"Is he a soldier or an airman?"

"First he was with the RAF, and now he is an American airman, but I haven't seen him in a long time, and I don't know anything about what he does."

"We should find out where he is and then I could write him a letter. My spelling is quite good," Michael declared solemnly.

Henry and Minette smiled. "I think that is an excellent idea."

"I do, too. And Lizzy can draw a picture for him." Michael settled back against the car seat and gazed out the window. Henry reached across the gear shift and gently squeezed Minette's hand.

The City Chronicle
November 23, 1944

Tattletales by Sharon Chatsworth

On this Thanksgiving Day, it is fitting that we follow the wise advice of our president, Franklin D. Roosevelt, and "give thanks with special fervor to our Heavenly Father for the mercies we have received individually and as a nation and for the blessings He has restored, through the victories of our arms and those of our allies, to His children in other lands."

I know that in the Augustus household special thanks will be given for the safe arrival in the city of Minette Rothchild Augustus and her grandson Michael Augustus. It will lift the spirits of the entire family to have them safely back in the city.

Chapter Three

Mary Elizabeth sat close to her father's bed, listening to his labored breathing and waited for him to wake. The past few days had been difficult and the doctor had warned them that Walter was dying. She stroked his hand gently, remembering the good times and letting the bad times go. She loved her father and knew that he loved her, perhaps not the way he had loved her brother Michael, but enough. Walter opened his eyes, and she saw the recognition in them. She smiled at him and felt his fingers tighten around hers.

"Boys?" he whispered.

Mary Elizabeth patted his hand and smoothed back the hair from his forehead. "Sam will be here soon," she assured him. "Minette has arrived with John's children. They will come to see you when they have rested."

"Michael?"

"Yes, Michael and Elizabeth."

Walter smiled slightly. "Sylvia?" he asked.

She understood and answered, "Sylvia doesn't know they are home. We will tell everyone that Elizabeth is a war orphan. Michael only knows that Valerie was Elizabeth's mother. He doesn't understand that John is her father."

"Someday," Walter murmured.

"Yes," Mary Elizabeth agreed, "someday he will know, but, with any luck, when he learns the truth, he will be old enough to understand."

"John?" Walter asked.

"I don't know where he is, but Minette feels sure he is safe and I trust her. Rest now, and I'll bring the children in a bit so you can see them."

Walter obediently closed his eyes and drifted off to sleep, his hand still clutching hers. Mary Elizabeth sighed. *Another secret*, she thought. *This family is built on secrets and lies.*

Minette explained to the children that their great grandfather was ill, but he would like to see them and welcome them home to the United States. Michael listened gravely and then asked, "Do I remember him?"

"You might. He certainly remembers you."

"He was very old, and my mother was mean to him. Annie told me not to listen, but when we came home from the park he was leaving, and he told me I was a good boy and gave me a wooden elephant."

"Goodness!" Minette exclaimed. "You have an excellent memory."

Michael nodded solemnly. "If the elephant is still in my room, I'll give it to Elizabeth. I'm much too old to play with it now, and it is a lovely elephant."

Minette stooped and hugged Michael. "You are a wonderful boy, Michael. Come"—

she took their hands—"let's go and see your great grandparent."

Walter awoke as the children entered his room. Mary Elizabeth rose from her chair and went to them, ready to hug them both, but sensing Michael's hesitation she stopped and smiled at them instead. "I'm so happy to have you home, Michael. We've all missed you so very much. As soon as you are settled I want you to tell me all about living in Wales." She touched Elizabeth's shining dark curls. "And you must be Elizabeth. You are very pretty."

Elizabeth ducked behind Michael and clutched his shirt in her hand. "She's a bit shy, ma'am," Michael stated.

"That's quite all right. You don't need to call me madam, Michael. When you were small you called me Aunt Mary and that will do nicely."

"Yes, ma'am—I mean Aunt Mary. Should Lizzy call you Aunt Mary, too?"

"Of course she should, darling. Now come and say hello to your great grandfather."

The children drew near to the bed, and Walter gathered his strength and managed a smile. "Welcome home, Michael, and welcome to America, Elizabeth." He paused to catch his breath and then continued, "I hope you'll both be very happy here."

"I'm sure it will be fine, sir. Grandmother Minette says that we will live in my old house and when my father comes home from the war he will live with us." Michael nodded sagely. "That will work until Sylvia comes back. She really doesn't like me, you know, so then Lizzy and I will have to find another place to live."

Walter was so astounded by this calm, mature speech that he was unable to think of an appropriate response. Mary Elizabeth looked to Minette and Minette managed to say, "Michael,

I'm sure that Sylvia loves you very much. She's your mother."

"I know. But sometimes mothers are too busy to like their children."

Looking for a way to get past this uncomfortable conversation, Minette said, "I think it is time for us to go home and settle in. Say good-bye to your great grandfather."

Michael leaned down and kissed Walter on the cheek. "Good-bye, Grandfather. I hope you feel better tomorrow." He drew Elizabeth forward and whispered to her. Obediently, Elizabeth kissed Walter's cheek. Walter sighed and closed his eyes.

"Goodness gracious!" Mrs. Peters exclaimed. "Look at you!"

Michael laughed. "I know you! Do you remember me?"

"Well, of course I do. Even though you've grown a foot and you sound like a proper Brit."

Michael laughed again and drew Elizabeth forward. "This is Elizabeth. She's mine, and she is going to live with me forever."

"Is that right?" Mrs. Peters smiled. "Do you remember the way to the kitchen? I've made some of those oatmeal cookies you like and Elizabeth looks hungry."

Michael looked worried and he turned to Minette. "May we go to the kitchen?" Minette nodded. "Sylvia doesn't like me to eat in the kitchen."

"*Nom d' un...*," Minette muttered. "Go with Mrs. Peters and enjoy your cookies. I'm sure your mother won't mind."

Duncan took control of the luggage, and, with the children in the care of the housekeeper, Minette had time to phone Sam.

"We have arrived. And I have a million questions. What in the world has been happening here? Where is Sylvia and why does Michael think she doesn't like him?"

"It's a long story, Minette. Too long for this phone call. Get some rest tonight, and I'll be by in the morning and we can talk about everything."

"Don't try to protect me, Sam. I need to know the truth."

"I agree, but, please, can we have this conversation face-to-face? I promise I'll be there at nine tomorrow morning, and we'll talk then."

Minette sat and stared at Sam as he filled in the family history. He started with Michael's birth and the fact that John was not his biological father, how Sylvia had tricked John, and then how they had been unable to divorce due to the terms of her father's will. How separately they had lived their lives, how Sylvia's drinking had escalated and resulted in her neglect of and then injury to both Michael and Annie, and, finally, Sylvia's nervous breakdown and hospitalization after the accident where she had been responsible for the death of her childhood friend Beau Campbell.

"Oh dear, *comment cela a-t-il pu arriver?*" Minette exclaimed, and then noting Sam's face she returned to English. "How could this happen? I do not understand."

"It is sad," Sam said carefully.

"*Sad* hardly covers the situation, Sam. What in the world was John thinking to allow this to happen?" She sighed deeply. "Well, of course, he was not thinking. But now we must think and plan. The children must be protected and loved." Sam nodded and she continued, "Tell me more about Sylvia, is she getting better? Will she be able to come home soon?"

"Her doctors tell me that she doesn't want to come home, that she doesn't want to be a wife to John or a mother to Michael."

"*Mon Dieu*! What is wrong with that woman?" Minette waved her hand at Sam. "Never mind. It does not matter. Until John comes home, I will take care of the children here in this house."

Life in a home with children was always full and busy, but life in a home where everyone must get to know each other again was not only busy but confusing and often stressful. One afternoon in early December, Mrs. Peters spoke her mind to Minette, "Begging your pardon, Mrs. Augustus," she said, "but I think these children need to be with other children. As soon as the Christmas break is over they need to go to school. I'd suggest a new nanny for the children but they are not available. All of the young women are busy with war work and, even if you did find someone, Michael needs friends his own age."

Minette tilted her head, considering this. "Perhaps you are right. I was waiting for the children to feel at home and for John to contact us, but…. Yes, I think you are right."

The children's arrival had seemed to provide a tonic for Walter and his health rallied enough that the family was able to gather together on Christmas Day. As they bowed their heads to say grace, each member whispered their own prayers for Walter's health, for the health of Sarah, Sam and Helen's youngest child, for John's safety, and for the continuing success of the Allied troops.

The City Chronicle
January 1, 1945

Tattletales by Sharon Chatsworth

Where, oh where has Sylvia gone? Where, oh where can she be? This question continues to haunt the conversations of the socially active of our fair city as another holiday season has come and gone. While Mrs. Minette Augustus was seen enjoying the city with her grandson, Michael, his many cousins, and the war orphan she brought back from England, Sylvia was not spotted at any event or any party. Is the famous family hiding a secret?

Chapter Four

Minette joined the children in the kitchen for breakfast. It had become their custom to start each day in the warm, friendly room under the loving eye of Mrs. Peters. Minette dropped a kiss on each child's head and gratefully accepted a cup of strong black coffee.

Michael grinned. "Did you make a New Year resolution, Grandmother? Elizabeth and I did."

Minette could see that he was bursting with his news, so she nodded soberly and said, "Not yet, but perhaps I will. How do you know about resolutions? Did you make them in Wales?"

"Christopher told us. He said it's very important that you decide on a thing to do, and that if you do it you feel really good."

"That is certainly true, and the start of a new year is a good time to begin. Would you like to tell me your resolution?"

"Elizabeth and I have decided not to go to school. We will feel really swell if we study at home with you and Duncan and Mrs. Peters."

"*Mon Dieu*! That is an interesting resolution."

"I know, Grandmother. It will be so much better to stay here and so much easier for everyone." Michael nodded wisely, satisfied that he had resolved many issues.

"But what about making friends? For both of you, girls for Elizabeth and boys for you?"

"We are fine. And we have the cousins. They are our friends."

"They are, but they are much older than you and they all go to school."

"Not Sarah. She studies at home."

"True, but Sarah isn't strong enough to go to school. You are very strong, and I think you would like school very much."

"No. I made a resolution and I have to keep it."

"I don't think I can support that, Michael. Your father attended St. Paul's, and I'm sure that if he were here he would want you to go there, too. It's a very good school."

"No." He shook his head. "I have to stay here, with Elizabeth."

Suddenly, Minette understood, and she smiled gently at the somber boy. "You will only be away from eight in the morning until about four in the afternoon, and part of that time Elizabeth will be at her own school."

Michael considered this idea carefully. "I think she is too little for school."

"I absolutely agree with you, but remember how much fun you used to have with Annie?" He nodded. "Since we don't have a nanny, I've found a play group that she can attend three mornings a week, and the rest of the time I'll be with her, and I promise I'll take very good care of her." Michael thought on this. "Would you like to visit the play group?"

"I think that would be a very good idea." He smiled and turned to Elizabeth. "Finish your toast and then we can build a tower."

When the children were out of earshot, Mrs. Peters grinned at Minette. "You've got your hands full with that one. He's smart as a whip, and I've never seen a child so concerned about a sibling," she said.

The next morning, Minette and the children set out for the nursery school. It was only a few blocks from the house and the winter weather was mild, so they'd decided to walk. Elizabeth skipped along happily, one small mittened hand in Minette's and the other in Michael's. They made a charming picture, the well-dressed, beautiful older woman and the two happy children. But outside the tall brownstone building that housed the school, Michael stopped.

"This is a real school, Grandmother. Not a play group. It says so right there." He pointed to the words carved in the transom over the door. "See, it says, 'Miss Porter's School for Girls.' I told you, Elizabeth is too little for school." He scowled and planted his feet. Minette could see that he was ready to turn away and head home.

"Michael, you must learn to trust me. Yes, of course, it is a school for girls, but it is also a school that offers a play group for little girls so that they can begin learning. Now, come along." Minette turned impatiently and, taking Elizabeth with her, started up the stairs. Behind her, she could hear Michael muttering.

With a few quick steps, Michael caught up and took Elizabeth's hand again. "Valerie says it's all right, so I'm going to let Elizabeth see this place."

"Michael," Minette started to speak, ready to reprimand him for his words and his tone. She stopped herself and decided it would be better to confront him later. "Come along. We don't want to be late."

Back at the house, after Elizabeth was settled with Mrs. Peters in the kitchen, Minette drew Michael into the office. "Michael," she said carefully, "you are a wonderful big brother for Elizabeth."

He interrupted. "I'm not her real brother, Grandmother." That stopped Minette for a moment. How much did this child know? "But Valerie said she was mine and that I should take care of her."

"And you do take very good care of her, but sometimes you will need to let others take care of her. You need to go to your own school and learn about the world and make friends with boys your age." Minette knew she was avoiding the issue, but she had no idea how to explain the many tangled relationships existing in the Augustus family, so instead she focused on her other concerns. "I know you believe that Valerie gave you Elizabeth to care for, but you really mustn't tell people that Valerie is talking to you now."

"But, Grandmother, she does talk to me."

"Michael, it was very sad that Valerie was killed by a bomb on the very night that Elizabeth was born. But she was killed. And once a person dies, they really can't talk to you anymore."

"Valerie can." He crossed his arms and glared at her. "She says that most people can't hear her, but I can."

"Can you hear her now?'

"Of course, I can."

"Can you see her?"

"A little bit. Kind of like a dream."

"Do you see her now?"

Michael nodded and seemed to focus for a moment just off to the left of his grandmother. He smiled. "Valerie says for you not to worry, and that I'm perfectly normal."

Minette stared at him. If she hadn't been raised in a proper home, she was sure her jaw would have dropped. It made no sense that a seven-year-old child would declare himself "perfectly normal."

"I do think you are perfectly normal, but I don't think other people will understand if you tell them about Valerie."

Michael nodded slowly. "Okay, she says she agrees and I should be careful who I tell."

Lord, Minette thought, the ghost had more control over this child than she did; it was rather frightening. She'd need to find a doctor. Perhaps Sam knew of someone.

The children settled into their schools and life began to take on a routine that was a relief to Minette after the war years. She and Henry corresponded regularly, or as regularly as the war in Europe made it possible. Henry continued to check the hospitals in England for word of John, and Minette tried not to dwell on her son's absence. The war news was encouraging. But at home Walter's health was failing rapidly. Sam and Helen and Minette spent as much time as they could with him and Mary Elizabeth. In early February, Peter and Ruth returned from Arizona and the family were at Walter's side as he fell into a final sleep.

The City Chronicle
February 7, 1945

Tattletales by Sharon Chatsworth

While enjoying the balmy weather in the beautiful resort city of Yalta on the north coast of the Black Sea, our Allied leaders, President Franklin D. Roosevelt, Prime Minister Winston Churchill, and Premier Joseph Stalin, are forging a friendship that will last for generations. The news from the historic meeting taking place at the Livadia Palace is most encouraging. These powerful leaders are meeting to assure that the imminent victory in Europe will quickly be followed by our victory in the Pacific.

Closer to home, it is with a heavy heart that I report the death of Walter Augustus. His contributions to the war effort and to this city are too innumerable to list. His death occurred in the family home surrounded by his surviving children, Peter and Mary Elizabeth, his grandson, Samuel, and his devoted daughters-in-law, Ruth, Minette, and Helen. Perhaps now those elusive members of the family, grandson John and his wife Sylvia, will reappear.

Chapter Five

Peter and Mary Elizabeth Augustus stood on the steps of the church and watched as the casket was loaded into the hearse. The frigid wind whipped around the corner threatening to tear Peter's hat from his hand. Mary Elizabeth slipped her hand through the crook of his arm and Peter covered it with his own gloved hand. They understood each other and knew that the grief they each felt was tinged with relief. It had always been the two of them united in their need for approval from a father who chose neither of them as his favorite child.

Ruth joined her husband, Peter, and the three settled into the first car behind the hearse. The other mourners quickly moved toward their autos, switched on the headlights, and joined the cars proceeding to the cemetery. Vehicles stopped and allowed the procession to pass. Men removed their hats and women covered their hearts or crossed themselves. The long line of cars turned into the cemetery, through the ornate gates, and, following the hearse, arrived at the Augustus mausoleum. The three wide, shallow steps were piled with floral arrangements. The white granite stone angels glowed softly in the pale winter sun. As Peter helped first Ruth and then Mary Elizabeth from the car, he said, "It's actually very beautiful, isn't it?" Mary Elizabeth nodded and drew on her gloves.

"I assume I'll be buried here, too," she said. "There's certainly enough room for several more generations." Peter looked at his sister sharply, wondering about her health, but she didn't seem unduly sad, just thoughtful, and he decided that this wasn't the time to mention that he and Ruth had agreed to be buried in Arizona.

After the minister said a few words and a long prayer, all the generations of the family followed the casket into the crypt and watched silently as the casket was slid into place and the brass door was closed and locked. Elizabeth clung to Michael's hand, and Michael stayed close to Christopher, who was holding Sarah's hand. After another prayer, the children were allowed to leave and the adults remained for a final farewell. As they stepped outside, an old woman rolled down her window and watched them from a limousine that was pulled up close.

"Who is that?" Michael asked.

Christopher shrugged. "Some friend of great grandfather's, I suppose. Do you want to ride back to the house in our car?" Michael nodded. "Come on then. It's cold out here and Sarah needs to get out of the wind." As they climbed into the car, Michael turned to see the old woman still staring at him. He tried to smile politely but only managed a half-hearted wave of his hand.

Back at the house, the older children, Christopher, Peter, and Jennifer, spoke graciously to the guests and then were allowed to join the younger children in the library. As Christopher had promised, they were served sandwiches and cake. "So, Michael," Christopher asked when the others were busy with a board game, "do you see Elizabeth's mother all the time?"

Michael's eyes widened, and he was unsure of how he should answer. Grandmother Minette had warned him not to talk about Valerie. But this was Christopher, and he was pretty sure he could trust him. He shook his head. "Not all the time, just sometimes."

"Like now? Is she here?"

Michael looked around carefully. "No. Why?"

"I'd like to see her or at least talk to her. Tell me what she looks like. Can you see through her?"

Peter looked up from the board game. "Or does she look like Casper, the friendly ghost?"

"I don't know who that is," Michael said. "I've never heard of Casper."

"He's in a book," Jennifer chimed in. This conversation was much more interesting than the game. "We saw a cartoon at the movies last week. He was cute and very sweet. He just wanted to make friends."

"I thought it was dumb," Peter said. "There's no such thing as ghosts!"

"That's 'cause you're dumb," Jennifer tossed back. Michael relaxed as the scrabbling moved the conversation away from Valerie and ghosts.

Late in the evening, Peter and Mary Elizabeth sat in that same library, sipping at glasses of brandy and talking quietly. Their childhood had been clouded with their father's obvious preference for Michael, their younger brother, John's father, and even now in their seventies they weren't sure what had gone wrong, why they had never been good enough.

"Do you think father ever loved us?" Mary Elizabeth asked. She avoided Peter's eyes by looking into the fire. They had not talked openly with one another about their shared childhood in more than forty years. "Remember when you came to my college graduation?" Peter nodded. "You said then that we would have to make our own families since we didn't have one."

"I was drinking that night."

"I know, Peter, but it was true. Michael had just died. Mother was already ill, and even though she had loved us as best she could, she never was a match for father. I understood why they didn't attend the ceremony, but did you know that neither of them ever even said congratulations or asked what I wanted to do after college?" She spun the glass and watched the fire flickering through the amber liquid. "I was just as smart as you, as Michael, as anyone. I wanted to join the company. I wanted to work in the family business, but instead I moved back home and took care of mother for twenty-five years until she died."

Peter stared to speak, and she held up her hand to stop him. "You had joined the law firm, married Ruth, and had a son. You were making the life you'd told me to make, but I was afraid that if I didn't do what father wanted, he would never love me. And, you know what, he never did. I wasted my whole life waiting for that love."

"I've thought about this a lot, Mary Liz, and I don't think he even knew what a terrible father he was to you and me. From the time Michael was born, Mother's health was failing, and, for whatever reason, he doted on Michael. I think Mother loved us, but, like you said, she was never very strong."

They both stared into the fire for a few minutes, remembering the past and then Peter refreshed their drinks and said, "I don't think Michael died the way we've always been told."

"What?"

"I really don't. Somehow the story of his death never made sense to me. I think something is missing."

"Like what?"

"This may sound crazy, but I think I remember the night Michael came to our house." He poured himself more brandy and continued, "I saw Walter bring the baby into the house and give it to Mother."

"But…".

"I'm sure I remember that. Mother told us the next morning that we had a new brother and that the stork had delivered him in the night. I tried to tell her that I'd seen Walter bring the baby in and not a stork, but she was very upset and told me I must have been dreaming, and that I must never tell anyone about my dream."

"Maybe you were dreaming. You were only about five years old."

"I was almost six, and I liked to sit on the stairs at night after I was supposed to be asleep because there was enough light there to look at books. Mother had been reading to us from *The Court of Oberon* and I would look at the pictures and tell myself the story. And that's what I was doing when Michael arrived. I wasn't asleep."

Mary Elizabeth sighed. "But if that's true, where did Walter get a baby?"

"I think Walter was Michael's father, but I have no idea who the mother might be. I just don't believe it was our mother. When mother was very ill she told me that she knew many secrets. I wish I'd asked her more."

"Those last few weeks, she talked about secrets all the time, but I thought it was the pain and nothing she ever said made me think of Michael or his birth."

"Did she ever talk about his birth?"

"Of course not, Peter. She never talked about private matters." She made a face and shrugged. "I'm an unmarried daughter. It wouldn't have been appropriate. You and I are Walter's children too, so why was Michael the only one he loved? The only child he seemed to care about or even want."

"Michael was certainly wanted," Peter agreed, "and perhaps when we were born we were too, but after Michael was born, Walter stopped loving us and seemed to forget that we were even his children. And I don't think he was the least bit concerned with Mother's feelings. As I remember it, they were perfectly civil to one another but never loving."

"Well… As I remember it, they barely spoke at home, and when they did, it was usually Mother telling him what you and I were doing and him asking for news of Michael. By the time you entered high school, I think Mother had quit telling him anything, and they were living completely separate lives, at least at home. In fact, here in this house, it was as if we were two separate families, Walter and Michael and Mother and us."

"If he had a baby with another woman why didn't Mother leave him? Do you think she was unhappy?" asked Peter.

Mary Elizabeth sipped and said carefully, "Women never left their husbands back then. It wouldn't have been possible. I certainly wasn't aware that she was unhappy, but by the time we were teenagers she did withdraw from the family."

"She was sick," Peter added.

"Not in the beginning. As an adult, I can guess that she must have been unable to have more children and that she accepted that Walter would look for satisfaction somewhere else."

Peter started to protest, but she ignored him and continued, "Women are taught that men need sex, Peter." She grinned. "Don't look so shocked. I know about sex even though I'm an old maid. And just because she accepted it, I'm sure it broke her heart. Don't you remember how much fun we'd have when it was only the two of us doing something with her? If you are right about Walter being the stork that brought Michael, Michael's presence must have been a constant reminder to Mother of Walter's affair. I never even considered that

Michael was not their child, but it makes sense of a lot of things, doesn't it?"

"Yes. And if they lied about his birth, why not about his death?" She nodded she was listening, and Peter continued, "I've thought about this a lot and for a long time. I even tried to talk to Mother about it once. She didn't deny anything but just brushed it aside saying I should let 'sleeping dogs lie' and that what was in the past was best left there."

"I know Michael was high spirited," Mary Elizabeth protested, "but he didn't really do anything wrong. When he died in France, it was just a terrible accident, a tourist robbery that went bad."

"I don't think so, and I have some good reasons to believe that something else happened. Do you know why he was in France?"

"Of course, I do. After he graduated from high school, Walter thought a year abroad would help him determine what he wanted to study in college."

"That sounds nice, but there is more to that story. Michael was drinking, cutting classes, and getting into brawls all over the city. Walter was covering up for him, always excusing his behavior, but it was getting harder to keep his name out of the paper."

"How do you know that?" Mary Elizabeth asked.

"When I was in high school I was always hanging around the courthouse, watching trials, and I became good friends with Jerry McGuire and his partner. They were young attorneys, only a few years older than I was, and not only was I an appreciative audience, I had enough pocket cash to buy them coffee. So when I was back in the city after law school, we picked up our friendship, and one night I realized that some of their stories about rich boys getting away with vandalism were about Michael. When

I asked, they hesitated but then confirmed it. It seemed that it was common knowledge in the police force that when Michael Augustus was drunk and disorderly or throwing eggs or picking fights he was to be treated gently and returned to his home—no arrests ever—is what they said."

Mary Elizabeth considered this carefully. "So you think that was why he was sent to Europe?" Peter nodded. "And what do you think happened?"

"I've studied the newspapers that were published, both here and in Paris, around the date of Michael's death, and I can't find anything that mentions him by name except for his obituary. Don't you think that is strange?" She nodded. "It would seem to me that if a rich American playboy was murdered during a robbery in Paris that would have been a sensational news story both here and there. It would have provided fodder for weeks, first the murder, then the arrest and trial of the perpetrator. Michael's name and picture would have been splashed across the front page multiple times. And the obituary says that Michael died from a "sudden illness." Not exactly how I'd describe someone murdered overseas during a botched robbery."

"Walter is"— she corrected herself— "*was* very powerful. He must have managed to suppress the story."

"Even Walter wasn't all-powerful. Suppressing a murder story in a foreign country would have been impossible, or at least very hard, even for him. Someone powerful in France would have had to be involved."

"But if he wasn't murdered, what did happen?" They sat in silence considering the implications of Mary Elizabeth's question. "If he died of a 'sudden illness', what was it? Why wouldn't they talk about it?"

"I've thought about that a lot and I think he was murdered, but I think he was murdered doing something that Walter chose not to acknowledge, because if he'd been murdered in a robbery, Walter would have been obsessed with finding the murderer and bringing him to justice. Something else happened."

"Does it really matter how he was killed? I'm much more interested in where he came from."

"Perhaps it doesn't matter, but sometimes when you start at the end of the story you can figure out the beginning. It's a mystery that has puzzled me most of my life and I would like to know the answer."

"What about his marriage to Minette? Surely that was mentioned in the papers, if not here in Paris." Peter shook his head. "Did you look for the marriage records in France?"

"I did. But even though I found nothing, it doesn't really mean anything. They were married in a small village in the south of France, and the priest should have recorded the marriage in the parish records and then sent it on to the government. But it isn't unusual for the record keeping to be inaccurate."

They sat quietly for a few minutes, each lost in their own memories of their childhood, of their parents, and of their brother Michael. Everyone who might know the truth firsthand was gone, and they were both aware that Walter, who valued the family name above all else, would certainly have kept the secret of his youngest son's birth and death. Perhaps it was too late to solve this mystery after all.

The City Chronicle
April 13, 1945

Tattletales by Sharon Chatsworth

We, at *The City Chronicle*, join with the nation in grieving the death of President Franklin Delano Roosevelt. For twelve years, in both war and peace, he was our leader. We will remember this gallant, fearless man, not only for his strong, brave leadership, but also for his charming smile. Americans will not forget the jut of his chin, the angle of his cigarette holder, or the words of courage that he gave to us during his first inaugural address: "The only thing we have to fear is fear itself." Rest in peace, Mr. President.

Chapter Six

Sam sat in his office, feet on the desk, chair tipped back, and thought about the state of the world, his wife and children, his parents, and the mess John had made of his life. At least the news from Europe was good. Well, *good*, he acknowledged, wasn't the right word, but certainly the war news was encouraging. The Allies were winning in both Italy and Germany. But there were disturbing stories printed every day about Nazi crimes against citizens. This morning's paper had carried a horrible story about the liberation of two concentration camps, Buchenwald and Belsen. It was hard to believe that anyone could treat another human being in such a manner. He worried that John might be held as a prisoner of war.

Despite how mad he was at him, Sam acknowledged to himself that John was his best friend. It was a blessing that Minette had been able to find the kids and bring them home, and that she was willing to live in John's house and care for them. At first, Helen had suggested that they come to live with them, but Minette had been right to insist that they would be better off settled in a house they could learn to call home. His own children were growing up so fast. Christopher was eighteen, graduating this year and still crazy about airplanes. Sam worried that he would enlist and be caught up in the war. If he did, Sam knew that it would break Sarah's heart, to say nothing about how awful he and Helen would feel. Chris had been Sarah's protector and friend since birth, and they were especially close. His youngest was still fragile, and the doctors held out little hope that she would live a full life. She was too frail to attend school, and so she was taught at home, but each of her siblings came directly to her each afternoon and told her everything that had happened in their day, good or bad. Sarah thrived on these stories and longed to join them at school.

Overall, Sam knew that their family had been extremely fortunate. Only John and he had been of an age to fight in this horrible war, and with John gone and Walter's failing health, the government had needed him to run AmCo. He'd done a good job of it too, even if he had to say so himself. He was a lawyer, not a businessman, but when John disappeared, he'd put his practice on hold and done what needed to done, and it was almost embarrassing how much money the family had made since America entered the war. Sam swung his feet off the desk and got back to work.

At seven o'clock, when the phone rang on his desk, he reached for it, expecting it to be Helen checking on when he would be home. "Hello, Beautiful," he said cheerfully. When silence answered him, he repeated, "Hello?"

"Mr. Augustus?" a hesitant voice asked.

"Yes, this is Samuel Augustus. Who is this? The office is closed."

"You don't know me, but this is Sandra Davis. Your grandfather was a friend of my mother." The woman's voice paused and when

Sam made no comment, she hurried on. "I'm calling because I really need to talk to you about a very private matter."

Sam remained silent. He'd just been counting his blessings and now this. It must be something about John since Sylvia was still locked up in the sanitarium. Those were the only two he knew that seemed to have "private matters" that needed discussion.

The quiet lengthened and then the voice continued, "I need to speak with you soon. Please."

Sam considered her request. She sounded educated, older perhaps, or at least not young, and a little desperate. It was strange to get a call after hours. "I suggest you call back during business hours, and my secretary will give you an appointment."

"No, she won't. I've been calling for days, and she just says you are too busy or not available. I waited tonight until I saw her leave

and then I called because I must speak to you."
She rushed on. "I know I sound crazy, but I'm
not, honestly. I just need to speak with you."
Something in her voice kept Sam on the line.
"Please don't hang up. Just give me a minute."

"All right, you have a minute. What is
this about?"

"My mother is Susan Davis. She is very
ill. She has made a request that I want to honor
if it is at all possible, and if it is true."

"You are making no sense, Miss Davis,
and your minute is running out."

"She told me an amazing story about
your grandfather. I believe her story and..."

"My grandfather is dead." He
interrupted. "I'm going to hang up now." And
he did.

With his work disrupted, Sam decided to
quit for the night. Riding the elevator down, he
considered the strange call and wondered what
Helen would make of it. Exiting to the street,

he glanced around but didn't see anyone lurking about. The days were getting longer, but it was quite dark as he strode quickly to his car, his key in his outstretched hand. As he slid the key into the lock, a woman appeared on the opposite side of his vehicle.

He sighed. "I suppose you are Mrs. Davis." She looked quite normal, probably at least fifty, maybe early sixties. There was nothing threatening in her appearance.

She nodded. "It's *Miss* Davis," she corrected, "but yes. I'm sorry to accost you this way, but I really must talk to you. Please just listen for a minute," she pleaded.

When Sam didn't speak, she rushed on. "My mother says she gave birth to a child, a boy, in 1893 and that your grandfather was the father of that child. She knows her son died as a young man, but when Mr. Augustus died, she attended his funeral, and it brought back many memories and renewed her regrets. She is dying now herself, and she would like to know what happened to her son."

"Good God!" Sam shook his head slowly. She had to be referring to his Uncle Michael, John's father, but a man he and John had never known. He remembered his conversation with Walter the night John first admitted to his love affair with Valerie. There would have been no reason for Walter to lie to Sam about Michael's mother. Walter had said she died in childbirth, he was sure of that. "That is the most preposterous story I've heard in a long time. Whatever it is you think you are doing, I've listened to your story, I'm leaving now, and I don't want to be bothered by you or anyone in your family again."

Sam had kept his promise to Walter and had never told anyone about their conversation. He was sure that with Walter's death, he was the only one who knew the truth about Michael's death and that Michael and Minette had never been married. However, as quickly as he thought that, he realized that Minette knew the truth and perhaps she had told John. *Damn!* He struck his hand hard on the steering wheel. Once again, the family lies threatened to be revealed. If he heard from that Davis woman again, he'd have to do something.

The visit from Miss Davis kept Sam tossing and turning all night. Helen asked what was wrong, but he couldn't tell her. He'd promised Walter that he wouldn't tell anyone. Finally, he came to the conclusion that he needed to talk to Minette. After all, since she must know at least part of this story, he wouldn't be breaking his promise. At last, he was able to fall into a brief, heavy sleep.

In the morning, he rose early and drove directly to John's house. He parked and strode into the park where he paced around and around the paths until he saw the children leaving for school with Mrs. Peters. When the coast was clear, he crossed back to the house and rang the bell.

Minette opened the door and her happy greeting was erased by the look in his eyes. She opened the door wide and gestured for Sam to enter. "What's wrong, Sam?"

Minette listened quietly as Sam revealed his knowledge that Michael had been born out of wedlock to Walter and perhaps to this Susan Davis.

Minette sat with her hands clasped together in her lap. She gazed at Sam but didn't seem to see him. He explained when and where Walter had told him about Michael's birth and that Walter had said Michael's birth mother was dead and yet this Sandra Davis had been very convincing. He hesitated, unsure if he should admit that he also knew that Michael had never married her. Minette raised her head, straightened her back, and spoke. "I think it is quite possible that this woman gave birth to

Michael. Walter was a very powerful man for a very long time. I'm sure that Michael's birth records state that he was born to Walter and Edith the same way that he was able to provide a marriage certificate for Michael and me so that John would be a legitimate child.

"Walter wasn't evil, Sam, but he was very protective of his family, and he went to great lengths to assure that any secrets would remain secret. And..." She hesitated. "...I think we have to respect his wishes. What does this woman want? Why is she coming forward now?"

Sam shook his head. Once again, Minette had shown an impressive ability to cut to the heart of the matter. "I only spoke to the daughter. I really didn't believe her story, and I was actually quite rude. Perhaps we'll never hear from them again."

"That's wishful thinking, Sam. If the woman you met is telling the truth, she wants to help her mother and you can expect to see her again. Perhaps…" She paused and then continued, "I should meet with Miss Davis or maybe we should talk to her together and find out what she really wants."

Sam agreed that if he was contacted again he would arrange a meeting and Minette would be included, and so it was no surprise when Sam called late that afternoon and said that he had agreed to a lunch meeting with Miss Davis the next day. Entering the restaurant a few minutes early, Minette surveyed the waiting patrons and settled on a middle-aged woman dressed in a grey flannel suit.

She approached her. "Miss Davis?" At her nod, Minette continued, "I'm Mrs. Minette Augustus." Cautiously, the two women appraised each other.

Sandra knew about Minette Augustus from the gossip column and from reading about local events in the paper, but the woman she was gazing at seemed normal and approachable, not at all like a society matron. If it weren't for the slight French accent, Minette seemed completely ordinary.

"Sandra Davis. Mr. Augustus said you would be joining us." They shook hands and then followed the waiter to a table.

Neither woman knew how to start the conversation, so they busied themselves with the menus until Sam arrived. They ordered quickly and as soon as they were alone Sam demanded that Miss Davis repeat her story and tell them what she wanted.

She complied and ended by saying, "My mother is seventy-four years old. After Mr. Augustus's funeral she was very upset and told me about her past. She knows that both her son and Walter's wife died long ago, and now with Walter gone she wants to know what really happened to her son. I don't believe there can be any harm in granting her wish. Mother gave the baby up for adoption the moment he was born, and she doesn't intend to make trouble, nor do I. My mother has told me about her affair with Mr. Augustus and how it ended. Mother told me about the child named Michael Augustus who was my half-brother but who died before I was born. I believe her when she says that she kept her part of the bargain and never contacted Mr. Augustus or Michael but, now she just wants to know how and why he died so young." She folded her hands and waited calmly.

Minette looked at Sam and then down at the silver. She picked up a fork and fiddled with it. "I am Michael's wife." Sandra nodded. "He died in France only days after we were married. I was only seventeen and pregnant. My brother killed him in a rage." Minette heard both Sam and Sandra gasp, but she hurried on. "My brother served his time in prison and he is dead now, too. There really isn't any more to the story than that. Tell your mother I am sorry for her pain, but there is really nothing more." She laid the fork carefully on the linen cloth and bowed her head.

Sandra reached out and laid her hand over Minette's. "I'm sorry, too, but there is more. Mother would like to see her grandson and great grandson before she dies. She really doesn't want to cause pain or trouble, but you can certainly understand that she wants to know that the son she gave to the Augustus family was loved and happy."

Sam snorted. "That's a mighty big *more*. What gives your mother the right to interfere with this family? She surrendered the baby. Walter and Edith adopted him. His son and grandson never met him and never will. What in the world could seeing them provide?"

"Peace," Susan said quietly, "simply peace. She needs to know that she did the right thing all those years ago. She needs to forgive herself."

Minette wiped tears away from her eyes and rose from the table. "Let us think about this, Miss Davis. I never knew that Michael was adopted until Sam told me your story, and I need a few days to decide what to do. Surely you can understand that?"

Sam rose, too, and escorted Minette out of the restaurant. When he returned to the table, he was surprised to see the distress on Sandra's face. "It never occurred to me that the family didn't know that Michael was adopted. I'm so sorry to have upset Mrs. Augustus. I told my mother that they might not want to see the birth mother after all this time but..." Her voice trailed off. "Is it true that her brother killed Michael? My mother never hinted at such a thing."

"I'm sure Minette would not have told you it if it wasn't true. It was never reported in the papers, and for the sake of Michael's son and grandson I would hope that no one ever talks about it again. Surely, your mother would understand that even an old scandal like that would be bad for all concerned."

The two sat quietly. There didn't seem to be anything else to say, and yet there had been no conclusion to their meeting. Sam wanted to ask what she would tell her mother, but Sandra said nothing more and finally pushed back her chair and extended her hand. "Thank you," she said. "I'll be in touch."

The world news pushed thoughts of family prevarications from Sam's mind. In rapid succession, the Americans entered Nuremberg, German forces surrendered in the Ruhr, the Soviets reached Berlin, the Allies took Venice, Mussolini was captured and hanged by the Italians partisans, and on April 30 the news announced that Adolf Hitler was dead by his own hand. The debate raged as to whether he was truly dead or only in hiding.

Sam spent long hours at the office. The troops still needed the supplies AmCo delivered, and now more than ever he was truly running the corporation by himself.

The City Chronicle
May 9, 1945

Tattletales by Sharon Chatsworth

Yesterday's headline "IT'S OVER IN EUROPE" has brought joy to every heart in America and to our friends in Britain and the other Allied nations. Across our fair city, many turned out into the streets to celebrate the wonderful news, while others spent the day in quiet reflection.

For many, this is the end of six long years of misery and suffering. Some have a renewal of hope in a loved one's return from the front, but for numerous others who are mourning loved ones killed in service this moment of victory is bittersweet.

Ultimately, nothing will be quite the same again, but with victory in Europe comes a sense that sometime soon the world will right itself, and we will move forward into a world filled with peace.

Chapter Seven

With the victory in Europe, Sam felt he could take a few days off to spend a long weekend at home with Helen and the children. They hadn't talked about it, but Sam knew that Helen was as relieved as he was that Christopher would not be tempted to enlist following graduation. He would register for the draft, but with any luck, the country would not need his service. Even though the war in the Pacific continued, the family joined the rest of the nation in prayer and celebration.

Back at work on Monday, Sam's thoughts turned to John as they often did. Perhaps he would contact the family soon, or if something had happened, perhaps the government would let them know. It would break Minette's heart if he were to be declared dead, but it might be better to know. So with those family thoughts in mind, he felt no surprise when Sandra Davis called that afternoon. He took the call and agreed to arrange a time for her to meet once again with Minette and himself. *This time*, he thought, *I'll include Helen in the conversation.* Her ability to help him see all sides of a situation would be of benefit to them all.

On Thursday, they gathered in his office and if Sandra was surprised to have Helen included, she didn't show it. Once again, she pleaded her case for allowing her mother to meet her grandson and great grandson. It was Helen who spoke first. "As a mother myself, I certainly understand your mother's desire to find closure, and if John were home it would be up to him to see her or not. But John isn't home."

Minette stood and paced to the window. She gazed down at the city and then turned back to the group. Her face was drawn and sad. "I think I need to meet your mother. I've thought of little else since our last meeting, and

I believe that I owe her an explanation of her son's death." Sam started to speak, but she waved him to silence. "As a mother myself, I understand that the 'not knowing' is much harder than the 'knowing.'"

Minette's visit with Susan Davis was easier than anyone had expected. The older woman sat quietly and listened carefully to all that Minette shared with her. Tears shone in her eyes as she reached out and took Minette's hand. "Thank you, dear. I know it was hard for you to come here. It is good to hear the truth about my son after all these years. I was twenty-two, and I thought I loved Walter. I was so excited to be pregnant, and I was sure that he would marry me as soon as he could be free from his family. The birth was very hard and the midwife thought I would die, so she gave the baby to Walter. When I didn't die, he came back and told me that his wife would raise the child as her own, and he made me promise that

I would never tell anyone that I was the mother of his child. I realized what a selfish man he was, but I didn't feel that I had any choice. It was his child, and I had no means of support. I never saw Walter again. I kept the promise not to tell, even when I married and gave birth to Sandra. But I never forgot my first child. I read every piece of news I could find about the Augustus family and saved every picture that included Michael. I told no one anything, but Sandra found my box of memories when she moved me here to her house."

Minette sat holding the old woman's hand in hers. They were quiet for a long minute, and then Minette said, "My son, John, looks a bit like you. I'm sure if he were here he'd come to meet you but…" Susan patted her hand. "Would you like to meet your great grandson?" The gratitude that shown in her eyes was all the answer Minette needed. "We'll come back tomorrow then."

Michael was willing to skip school for the day and go to visit someone with his grandmother, but he wasn't quite sure why they were visiting this person. He only knew it seemed to be very important to grandmother. She'd told him that it was a friend of the family who was very ill but nothing about why he was included in the visit.

When they reached the Davis townhouse, Michael shook hands politely with Sandra and followed her to the sickroom. The woman in the bed seemed very old to Michael and he hesitated a moment as they approached the bed, but she smiled warmly and extended a hand.

"I know you," Michael said. "You came to great grandfather's funeral." She nodded. "I'm Michael Augustus," he said politely. "It is a pleasure to meet you Mrs. Davis." He took her hand in his and held it gently. Then he turned to Sandra and Minette and said, "Could we be alone for a minute?" Sandra looked at Minette questioningly. Minette shrugged, and the women agreed to leave the room.

"I think I know something, Mrs. Davis," Michael said. "Do you want me to tell you?" Her steady gaze searched his eyes and she nodded. "When Grandmother asked me to come with her today I didn't know why, but now I can tell that you wanted to meet me. I wish I was your real grandson, but I don't think I am." He paused and thought over his next statement. "Valerie told me I should come here today. She said that you are very ill and that you are afraid but that you don't need to be. Valerie says that everything will be all right."

"Who is this Valerie?" she asked softly.

"I think she's a ghost." Michael studied the woman's face but continued when he saw only interest and not disgust at such an idea. "She died when Elizabeth was born, and now she helps me take care of Elizabeth. And sometimes she tells me things I need to know, like now."

"Is she here now?" He nodded. "Will she stay with me?"

Michael tightened his grip on Susan's hand. "Yes. Valerie says it won't be long."

"Thank you, Michael. You are a wonderful child and I know you will be a wonderful man. I would have been very happy if you were my grandson." Michael leaned down and gently kissed her forehead. She let go of his hand and Michael left the room.

Sandra looked in on her mother and was relieved at the peace she saw in her mother's face. She thanked them for coming and again promised to never repeat any of her mother's story to anyone. On the ride home, Minette asked Michael what he had talked about with Mrs. Davis, but he only said, "Nothing much, just stuff." When she asked if he had any questions, he shook his head.

Minette told Sam about the visit and admitted that she was still worried that the family's lies would not remain buried. Walter had always kept such a tight hold on the family that Sam was quite sure that the documents were all in order, but he agreed to double check.

After Walter's death, the contents of his personal safe had come to him, so he reviewed everything and then checked the city and state records to be sure that everything matched. He found a registered birth certificate for Michael David Augustus, stating that he was born to Walter and Edith on May 3, 1893; the immigration and citizenship documents for Minette Louisa Rothchild Augustus that stated she was the legal widow of Michael David Augustus with a wedding date of May 19, 1912 in Provins, France; and a death certificate for Michael, stating that he had died of influenza on June 25, 1912, again in Provins, France; and, last but not least, there was John's birth certificate showing his birth to Minette and Michael Augustus (deceased) on January 19, 1913. Everything was filed and dated and registered correctly. If the files were to be believed, everything was in order. Walter had done a fine job and it seemed that, with the death of Mrs. Davis, all these secrets were protected.

Chapter Eight

Dr. Osgood smiled as Sylvia entered his office. She was a beautiful woman despite her unwillingness to cooperate with treatment. He knew without checking her chart that Sylvia

Augustus had entered their care in 1940 after a terrible auto accident in which she had been responsible for the deaths of six people, one of whom was her friend, and five of whom were innocent children. In all that time, she always kept herself well-groomed but she had spoken rarely and only when in need of something, never in response to questions, whether they were simple, friendly questions or deeper, probing therapeutic questions.

Truly, it was sad when someone so beautiful retreated from the world in such a tragic manner. He gestured toward a chair, into which she sank gracefully, still without smiling or acknowledging his presence.

"Sylvia, I have spoken to your family about your lack of response to treatment and while I assure you that I understand that you feel unable to talk with me, I need to find a way to help you. It is my goal, as I am sure it is yours, to return you to your home and to your child. I have suggested that we begin a series of electro-shock treatments and your husband"—Sylvia's head jerked up, but the doctor, intent on his notes, didn't notice her response—"...no, not your husband, your cousin-in-law, Samuel Augustus"—Sylvia's head dropped again—"has given his permission to begin treatment immediately." He looked over his reading glasses and saw only Sylvia's usual calm gaze. "Do you have any questions?"

Mutely, she shook her head, and he rose from his chair and motioned for her to do the same. As she exited, he thought for a moment that she looked into his eyes but decided that it must have just been a trick of the light. She really was a baffling case.

As a member of the wealthy Augustus clan, she had had everything, and yet here she was committed to psychiatric care for well over four years. Her husband was said to be overseas, a member of the military, but surely someone else should have visited. A woman as beautiful as Sylvia Augustus must have friends. He'd check the record again, but he was certain that the only family contact had been through Samuel Augustus.

Sylvia returned to her suite. She'd played the silent game so long that she wasn't sure she could speak. Pushing open the French doors that opened from her sitting room onto the twisting paths and gardens that caused this place to look much more like an expensive hotel than a hospital, she drifted out to her favorite bench. The trees were covered in the fresh glow of summer leaves and several gardeners were busy tending flowers along the paths.

She lit a cigarette and drew the smoke deep into her lungs and exhaled slowly. Her thoughts tumbled about, and she considered her next move. After the accident, she really had been upset. But who wouldn't be? They'd thought she was so withdrawn that she didn't know what was going on, but she'd heard Sam say that if she hadn't been hospitalized she would have been charged with a crime. This was ridiculous, of course. It had been an accident after all; she hadn't wrecked the car on purpose. Not speaking had kept her safe. She'd been completely cooperative; she just hadn't found it necessary to talk. But not talking didn't mean that she wasn't aware of what was happening around her.

She knew that when patients had electro-shock therapy they changed, and she liked herself just the way she was. Maybe she would have to start talking to someone, certainly not the doctor, but someone who would tell them that she seemed to be improving without treatment. Her head was clear. It had been months since she'd actually swallowed the pills they gave her every day, and perhaps it was time to get out of here. Surely the threat of prison was past, and it would be lovely to see her friends and go shopping for some new clothes. It was, she admitted to herself, boring to live like this. She wondered why Sam was making the arrangements for her treatment instead of John. Perhaps he'd found a way to get a divorce. She could see one of the male attendants approaching her bench. Now was as good a time as any to get started.

"Good morning, Mrs. Augustus."

Sylvia lifted her gaze and smiled slightly. "Good morning, Jake."

He stopped and stared at her. Had she spoken? Had she actually said his name? "How are you this morning?" he said, watching her closely.

"Better, Jake. Much better."

The flustered attendant turned and fled back toward the office wing. There, Sylvia thought with satisfaction, that would get the doctors' attention and should make them reconsider shock therapy. She rose from the bench and returned to her room. She wanted to shower and put on a bit of makeup before the doctor came to talk to her again.

Minette opened the door at Sam's knock. She kissed him warmly on each cheek in the French manner and drew him in. She waved toward the dining room. "I thought we could talk in here. When you called I had Mrs. Murphy fix lunch for us."

Sam made small talk for a few minutes, asking about Michael and Elizabeth and commenting on the new president, Harry Truman, and the AmCo contracts that would change now that peace had been declared in Europe. Then, taking a deep breath and squaring his shoulders, he said, "Sylvia's doctor called me today. She's started talking again."

"Excellent!" Minette shook her clasped hands in a modified victory clasp.

"Are you sure? The doctor seemed to think that this was a very positive sign but only last week he had asked for permission to use electro-shock therapy and worried that she would never recover, and now he's saying that she may be released soon. What if she wants to come back to the city? What if she wants to live here, in this house?"

As Minette considered his words, her smile faded. "Well, of course, she will want to come home and be with her son. This is her home."

"I'm not sure she considers this her home, and I don't think she is anxious to be a mother. After you moved to Paris to care for your mother, Sylvia's lifestyle didn't include her child, and I doubt that she has changed. Drunk or sober, Sylvia will always do whatever she needs to do to get whatever she wants. And I think that she began talking again because she was tired of playing the 'sick' game. If she comes here, it will be for her selfish reasons and not because she misses Michael, not to be a mother to him, and certainly not to be a mother to Elizabeth."

Minette shook her head slowly. "That seems very harsh, Sam. I imagine the doctor will not release Sylvia until he is sure she is well." They sat silently musing over the possibilities.

Finally, Sam said, "John needs to come home. Somehow we need to contact him. This is his mess, and he needs to clean it up."

Finding John was a good idea, but there still seemed to be no trace of him. Sam tried to inquire through all the normal channels but since he didn't want the media to realize the family had no idea where John was now or where and what he'd been doing for the past three years, each inquiry rapidly met a dead end.

He spoke with Dr. Osgood each week and each week the news of Sylvia's rapid recovery made it apparent that the hospital would soon be ready to release her. In July, Dr. Osgood requested that Sam come down and meet with him and Sylvia. He assured Sam that Sylvia was ready and anxious to return to the city and to resume her role as a wife and mother; he was certain that her drinking would never again be a problem. Sam and Helen weren't so sure, but Minette argued that Sylvia deserved a chance to prove that she had changed.

And so Sam found himself on a train returning to the city with Sylvia. She tapped her cigarette impatiently against her lighter. Sam watched her, but when he didn't offer a light she flicked her own lighter and drew in a deep breath. "Is this how it's going to be, Sam?" She lifted one elegant eyebrow and cocked her head. "I know you don't like me, but I'm sure my loving husband would want you to be nice to me."

"Really? Is that what you think? Have you forgotten that your marriage was over? That neither of you wanted to be together?"

"Over perhaps, but I understand that there is still no divorce. And so, after a terribly difficult time brought on by the death of my friend Beau, so soon after the death of my father, I'm returning to my home and my child to await the return of my darling husband from the war." She inhaled deeply and released the smoke in a series of lazy rings. "It would be quite helpful if you could catch me up on the news from John, so that I can make a reasonable response when asked about his war record."

Sam turned to face her, and she flinched at the coldness of his look. "You can play any game you want, Sylvia, but you aren't fooling me. I know that you were drunk and caused the accident that killed Beau and those innocent children. I know that you played ill and mute to avoid jail and I take responsibility for allowing that. But from here on out, I won't cover for anything you do or say, if you begin drinking again I'll see that you are committed. I'll be watching everything you do and how you treat Michael and Elizabeth."

"Ah, yes, the little war orphan, my husband's bastard child," she said coldly. "I'm supposed to love her, I suppose."

"No one expects that. You don't even love your own child"—he held up his hand as she started to protest—"but you will be kind to both the children. Until John comes home, I am telling you that you will behave."

"Goodness, Sam"—Sylvia batted her eyes at him—"do you talk to your wife like that? I'm surprised you're still married."

"I mean it, Sylvia. You'll stick to the story we'll tell the press, and you'll stay out of trouble."

Christ, Sylvia thought. *How'd I get into this mess? All I wanted was a divorce and my inheritance from Daddy.* She lit another cigarette and gazed out the window. They ignored each other until the train pulled in. Then Sam politely took her arm and they stepped off together.

The City Chronicle
Headlines

Monday, August 6, 1945
**Atomic Bomb Dropped on
Japan:
Missile Is Equal to 20,000
Tons of TNT;
Truman Warns Foe of a "Rain
of Ruin"**

Wednesday, August 8, 1945
**Soviets Declare War on Japan
Invade Manchuria**

Thursday, August 9, 1945
Atom Bomb Hits Nagasaki

The City Chronicle
August 15, 1945

Tattletales by Sharon Chatsworth

I thought a bombshell of our own had exploded last night when it was reported to me that the lovely Sylvia A. is back in town! I haven't spotted her at any of the usual places, but if the rumor is true, I'm sure we'll soon be seeing her out and about. Now where oh where can the elusive John A. be? Enquiring minds want to know.

Chapter Nine

Sylvia was not pleased with the way her return was going. The household staff was nonexistent, only Mrs. Murphy was living in. A cleaner came to the house weekday mornings but did her work silently and ignored anything Sylvia requested; either the woman didn't speak English or was plain stupid. Sylvia wasn't sure which. When she'd requested a cup of coffee, whatever her name was hadn't even acknowledged her and then Mrs. Murphy had simply nodded and poured her a mug of coffee in the kitchen and said that that woman was here to help with the cleaning not to wait on the family. Without a driver, she was expected to take cabs or buses or even walk. Maybe she shouldn't have been so ready to leave that hospital. At least there no one used the war to excuse everything.

But worst of all were the children. Minette seemed to do all the childcare herself. She got the children up and off to school and was there when they came home in the afternoon. She ate with them and played with them and put them to bed. On the weekend, she was with them every minute. And now, Minette was suggesting that she'd like to return to her own townhouse. She'd had the nerve to say that she felt that Michael and Elizabeth would benefit from having a mother living with them instead of a grandmother.

Obviously, that was just an excuse. She just doesn't want to bother with them anymore. She probably wants a life of her own even though, Sylvia thought, *she's too old for much of a life, and what about me? I don't want to be stuck with these children either. Elizabeth isn't even mine for heaven's sake! God! I'd like a drink.* Sylvia lit a cigarette and stared at herself in the ornate hall mirror. She'd have to think of something. Perhaps it was time to get in touch with her friends.

Sam and Helen were enjoying a rare dinner out without any children. They were relaxed and happy, talking about this and that, laughing at their children's antics and planning for the future. They avoided discussing problems until dessert was served. Then Helen plunged in. "What about John's family? How is

Sylvia? I called and suggested lunch, but she didn't want to see me."

"Minette says the adjustment has been hard. Sylvia keeps to herself, stays away from Michael and Elizabeth, and doesn't understand why the house has so little help. Minette thinks it might be better if she moved out and Sylvia was forced to be a mother and the head of the household. But"—he took a swallow of coffee and shook his head—"I'm not so sure. I don't think she knows how to do either of those things. I don't think she's drinking or even going out yet, but until we know where John is I think those poor kids need Minette." Helen agreed, and she encouraged Sam to continue his support of the current arrangement.

"Surely," she said, "we'll hear from John soon."

As if in answer to her words, it was only a few days later that Sam's secretary popped into his office excitedly waving a magazine.

"Look at this!" She spread the copy of *LIFE* out to reveal a two-page spread of pictures. "Isn't that Mr. Augustus?" She pointed at a laughing airman, surrounded by other airmen, all seated around what looked to be a barroom table.

Sam quickly scanned the story about servicemen enjoying a hot shower, a comfortable bed, and a good meal at the Grand Hotel in Paris. He studied the picture carefully. It certainly could be John, but there were no names in the caption, just a statement that read, "American Airmen from the 4th Fighter Group enjoying a well-deserved evening out on the town."

"May I keep this?" he asked, knowing that Minette would be thrilled to see the picture if it was in fact John. He wondered how Sylvia would react.

Minette glowed when she saw the picture, sure that it was John, but Sylvia's reaction was pure, hot anger. "Look at him," she said, sputtering. "He's having fun. The war is over in Europe. Why is he over there instead of here where he belongs?"

While her question was purely rhetorical, Sam wanted to respond by saying, *He's there because you are here*, but he knew the truth wasn't that simple. In fact, John had disappeared first by going to England and then into the war because he was unhappy and because he didn't want to face his responsibilities to his family or to the family business. When Sylvia had gone "off the rails," he'd refused to return to the States and had left Sam to deal with everything. It was true that Valerie's death must have been horrible for him, but they weren't married and he was married to Sylvia, even if he hated her. Ad now, there were two children to consider.

Sam actually found it hard to believe that John could simply leave his children behind. The idea of running away from responsibility was abhorrent to Sam, but he said none of these things, neither to Sylvia nor to Minette. Instead, he said firmly, "If this is a picture of John, we should all rejoice that he is alive and well and pray for his safe return."

"*Oui*," Minette murmured.

"I need a drink," Sylvia said and when Sam frowned, she smiled at him impishly. "It's been a shock seeing my missing husband alive and well and having a good time in Paris. Surely I deserve a drink." When Sam didn't move toward the bar, Sylvia walked over and poured three small glasses of brandy. She handed one to Minette and, tipping her glass to touch the rim to Minette's glass, she waved toward the third glass. "Come on, Sam. Let's drink to John's safe return."

The month of August slipped by. Sam made a few enquires and while it seemed obvious that John was alive and well, he did not contact the family. Sylvia swept her hair up into the new topknot style and began to go out to luncheons and an occasional dinner. Minette stayed close to home and continued to supervise the day-to-day activities of the children. The new school year began and both Michael and Elizabeth settled happily back into their respective schools. Each day, Elizabeth waited impatiently for Michael to return home and then she never left his side until bedtime, and even then it was Michael who read her a story and tucked her in.

With the war in Europe over at last, Minette was thrilled to read news of how Paris was coming back to life, and she was happy to know that John had experienced at least one night in her birth city. Her friendship with Henry Smyth grew with each letter they exchanged. He kept her informed of the changes in London, entertained her with stories about the people he met each day, and never once did he fail to ask after the children and to assure her that John would be home soon. He'd volunteered to go over to Paris to look for John when she'd written about the sighting at the Grand Hotel, but Minette knew that too much time had passed between the picture being taken and printed to even think that John might still be in Paris. Instead, she assured him that they all believed that John would be home soon.

The City Chronicle
Headlines

PEACE AT LAST

September 2, 1945
Japan Surrenders, End of War!
Emperor Accepts Allied Rule;

MacArthur named
Supreme Commander

The City Chronicle
September 28, 1945

Tattletales by Sharon Chatsworth

If I hadn't seen it with my own eyes, I'd never have believed it, but I did see it! Last night, the mighty Augustus family was dining together at the beautiful Saratoga Lounge. And, hold on to your hats, I really do mean the *entire* Augustus family. John Augustus, resplendent in his Air Corp uniform, with the beautiful Sylvia on one side and his mother on the other, his son, Michael, Samuel Augustus with his wife and all five children, Peter and Ruth Augustus, Miss Mary Elizabeth Augustus, and last but not least, the delightful little war orphan that Mrs. Minette Augustus brought home from England.

Chapter Ten

You'd think, thought Sam, *that with the war finally over and John back home that life could return to normal. And perhaps*, he admitted to himself, *this is normal.* The Chatsworth woman had said as much about their family in the paper this morning. John was back in the States and Helen and the kids were happy and busy. His parents were on their way home to Arizona. *Yep.* He tilted his chair back. This was most likely the new normal. Maybe he could actually stop running this company and go back to being an attorney.

Helen smiled as she ran her hand over Sarah's hair. She noted the slight blue tint to her youngest daughter's lips but only said, "Finish eating, darling. Your teacher will be here soon." By now the dire prophesies made by the doctors for Sarah were a normal part of life in their household and Helen was determined to give Sarah the most ordinary childhood possible. She knew how much her six year old wanted to attend the "real" school with her brothers and sisters, but that just wasn't possible. Her health was much too fragile.

Sylvia stood in front of the full-length mirror and assessed her body. *Not too bad,* she thought. It was a good thing that she'd walked the hospital grounds every day and had stopped swallowing those horrible pills. *I really don't look four years older. I can tell my friends I just needed to get away and have time to myself. No one knows where I've been except the family, and they'll never tell.* Sometimes the need for Augustus family secrecy could actually be a blessing.

Minette folded Henry's latest letter and slid it back into the envelope. She smiled, thinking of the words she'd just read. He really was a lovely man, and she knew that if he actually came to the States, she'd be delighted to see him. These letters were the first courtship she'd ever experienced (her brief love affair with John's father hadn't included courtship), and she admitted to herself she was having a wonderful time. Perhaps it was time to move out of this house and back to her own. With John home, she wasn't needed here anymore, and if Henry really was planning a visit, she'd like to be able to entertain him in her own home.

Walter had been kind and very helpful. He'd certainly protected them, but she'd never felt that she could date anyone; there were just too many secrets and lies. Somehow, Henry felt right, like new possibilities were opening up to her. She decided she needed to talk to John as soon as possible and move back into her own home.

Michael and Elizabeth sat in the kitchen with Mrs. Peters. They shared a plate of fresh oatmeal cookies, dipping each bite carefully into their milk. Elizabeth spoke through a mouth full of crumbs. "Who is that man?"

"He's my father. I think he's very nice. I told you this," Michael explained patiently. "He's been away fighting the war, but now he's back. He's married to Sylvia. She's my mother."

"But Sylvia's not my mother, because my mother was killed in the war. Is he my father?"

"I don't think so, but you had a lovely mother," Michael said firmly. "Her name was Valerie and now you live with me."

Mrs. Peters cleared her throat and wiped a tear from the corner of her eye. The way Michael took care of Elizabeth was so sweet. "Come, children, finish up and then off you go. I need to start your dinner."

"But, Michael," Elizabeth said, "why isn't he my father?"

"Don't know, and I don't think it matters. Lots of children have no fathers because of the war."

"I don't think your mother likes me. Do you think he likes me?"

"I'm sure he would if you stopped asking questions. Come on. Let's go over to the park. I'll push you on the swings." He took her hand and led her out as she continued to chatter.

John sauntered into Sam's office, his manner was casual as he slumped down into a chair and reached for a cigarette. Sam grinned at him. "What's up, Cuz? Do you need to talk?"

He wasn't surprised that John had seemed lost at dinner last night. Returning to his family after the war would have been hard enough on its own, but he'd been gone four years without communicating with anyone in the family and before that it must have been at least a couple of years where he avoided his wife and son. For a second, Sam actually felt sorry for him, but then he remembered how selfish John had been, how he'd refused to come home when Sylvia went "off the rails," and how he'd hidden in the war instead of taking his place in the family. Sam sat patiently waiting until finally his silence drove John to speak.

"The last thing I expected was to find Valerie's child alive and well and living in my house, with Sylvia and Michael. When I rang that doorbell and Michael and Elizabeth opened the door I almost ran away." He covered his eyes and continued, "She looks exactly like Valerie. I knew immediately who she was, and I know I've been a complete idiot. My only excuse is that I went a little crazy when Val was killed in the Blitz. I thought I'd lost everything, and now I find I have a beautiful daughter, but I'm still married to Sylvia, and I just don't know what to do."

Sam paced across the office and gazed out the window. He considered his words carefully and spoke softly, "I don't believe that

Sylvia has changed but neither has her father's will. If you take Elizabeth to live with you and divorce Sylvia, she will lose everything except Michael, and I believe it will drive her back over the edge. Right now, everyone believes that Elizabeth is a war orphan that Minette rescued and that Michael is your son. Those kids have been everything to each other for five years, and they are very close. You need to consider their futures before you make any rash decisions or separate them. But I will admit that the company is stronger than ever, and you could afford to give Sylvia a decent amount to live on, so perhaps divorce is a possibility."

John nodded. "I don't really care anymore what the gossips think or say about our family. When I lost Valerie, I lost the love of my life and when I found her... our daughter... safe and well, it was like Valerie reached out and touched me. Mother says that I need to consider my next move carefully and I know she is right." He rose and crossed the room to gaze out at the city. "Did you know Michael thinks that Valerie talks to him?"

"I do. We all do. He may be only eight, but he is a fierce protector of Elizabeth, and it is hard to dispute his conviction."

"But that's crazy."

"Is it? Most children who have seen and heard terrible things find a way to cope and a way to explain what they have experienced. I think seeing the house explode and losing you caused Michael to find someone to help him cope with a situation that was far too complex. He was only a three year old himself and he felt responsible for a new baby. I think it is remarkable that he is doing so well. His teachers tell me he is very bright and much more mature than most boys. He has adjusted well to being a day boy at Trinity School and he is making friends. I'm sure that, in time, when he feels that he and Elizabeth are safe, he'll stop talking to Valerie. It's rather like having an imaginary friend, isn't it?"

Everything Sam had said made sense to John, and he knew that his mother felt much the same way. His reunion with Sylvia had gone more smoothly than he could have expected. Of course, there really hadn't been a reunion. He'd only been home a few days, and he hadn't spent any time alone with her. Sylvia hadn't been at the house when he arrived. Minette had been so excited to see him alive and well. Elizabeth had been such a huge surprise. Sam and his family had arrived in a flurry of hugs and questions that, by the time Sylvia walked in, her surprise at seeing him was lost in the general noise and rush. Although they'd been less than delighted to see each other, they'd managed to get through the evening. He'd caught up on sleep and then last night at dinner, they'd played the happy couple for everyone who stopped by to welcome John home.

"I'll be mustering out soon and then I'll be back. I know I've been a jerk, Sam. I want to make it right. Valerie would want me to raise Elizabeth. We were looking forward to her birth, and I know she would have been very disappointed in me these last five years, in the way I ran away. I know I owe a great deal to you for all you've done to protect me and the family and for the way you've managed AmCo."

Sam wanted to say that it had been no problem, but he couldn't bring himself to lie. Instead, he just shook his head and thought, *You don't know the half of it. The family's lies and secrets have not lessened with Walter's death. They are expanding and now, somehow, I've become the keeper of those secrets.*

The City Chronicle
January 30, 1946

Tattletales by Sharon Chatsworth

It's a late but Happy New Year in the John Augustus home today as it was reported by the family that John has been released from the military and will be returning to the family business as the Chief Executive Officer of AmCo Industries. Samuel Augustus will return to his position as Legal Officer. Sylvia Augustus has been seen more and more frequently partaking in the new post-war social scene and is reported to be looking forward to a visit to the White House.

Chapter Eleven

With John's imminent arrival back in the household, Sylvia knew that they needed to talk. Things couldn't go back to the way they were before the war. Too many people were already asking too many questions. They needed to either divorce or create a cover story and a life that others wouldn't question. The four years that she'd spent in Charleston needed to be accounted for. Fortunately, the family had covered John's absence and if Michael kept his mouth shut about Wales, it would be assumed by everyone that he had been with her in the south, waiting out the war. Of course, Minette had brought him and that girl back to the city months before she'd arrived, but they'd have to figure something out. The Augustus family's need for privacy might be working to her advantage and she thought it was about time.

As John started his travel home, his thoughts were much the same as Sylvia's, and so he called the house and suggested to Sylvia that she should come down to Washington, DC, where they could spend a couple of days planning the future. Sylvia jumped at the chance, certain that her ability to wrap men around her beautiful fingers would work best away from Minette, two noisy children, and the ever-present Sam.

A few days later, she stepped from the train wearing a refined, unadorned grey padded jacket with boxy square shoulders and a dark blue short, just below the knee, straight skirt. She'd been listening to her friends and knew that most women were making do with clothing from before the war or by having clothing made over to look new. She wanted to fit in, so she too had reused a suit to have this one created, but she hadn't been willing to compromise on her stockings. She was wearing gossamer-thin silk stockings with perfectly straight seams. Those nylons others were wearing were just too thick. Sylvia accepted the porter's hand and looked around for John. Instead, a young sergeant stepped forward and took her bag from the porter. "Welcome to DC, Mrs. Augustus. Captain Augustus will meet you at the hotel. He said to tell you he was held up in a meeting."

Sylvia smiled graciously and was pleased to see the young man blush. Her slight southern accent increased as she thanked him. "I'm sure you'll take very good care of me."

"Yes, ma'am," he stammered and blushed again as he handed her into the waiting car.

At the hotel, Sylvia was surprised to find that the room John had reserved was actually a two-bedroom suite. The bellman placed her bag in one bedroom, and she declined his offer to order food or drink and instead stepped out on the balcony to look at the lights of the capital and to wait for John. It wasn't that she didn't want a drink, she did, but she wanted John to believe that her drinking was merely social and completely under control.

When she heard a knock at the door, she turned and watched John enter. "Hello, darling," she drawled. "I take it this is a business meeting not a loving reunion."

John didn't react to the greeting or the tone. "Thank you for coming down, Sylvia. You are looking very well. I simply thought that we would be able to talk here and to make our decisions about the future without the family or that Chatsworth woman watching us." She nodded in agreement. "Would you like a drink?" She nodded again, surprised that he was offering. "Still gin and tonic?"

John crossed to the bar and mixed them each a drink. "I want to get out of this uniform and then we can talk. Make yourself comfortable." Sylvia stared after him as he entered the bedroom and closed the door. She held the cool glass up to the light and smiled her first full smile. If he didn't think of her as a drunk, maybe this would be easier than she'd thought. She set the glass on a table and turned to the other bedroom to change from her suit to a comfortable robe. They could stay in tonight and work things out. She'd drink slowly, and it would be all right.

Back in the living area, they sat in the comfortable lounge chairs and raised their glasses in a salute to each other. "So," John began, "how are the children and mother?"

"Everyone is very excited that you will be home to stay soon. Minette is talking about moving back to her own house to give us space. I think she is a bit tired of living with children. They keep her very busy." She smiled at him over her glass. "Is a divorce still out of the question, John?"

"Nothing has changed that would affect your father's will. But I'm wondering if we have changed? Are you dating anyone?" She jumped at his blunt question but shook her head. "Well, neither am I, and with Valerie gone, I have no interest in anyone else. I've been thinking this over for weeks now. I want to raise my child. I want her to live with me, and I don't want anyone to ever know that she was born before I could marry her mother. I want to give her the best life that I can. I'm willing to act as Michael's father, if you are willing to act as Elizabeth's mother."

Sylvia finished her drink and waved for a second. John filled both their glasses and waited for her response. "How do you think that will work, John? You are Michael's father of record, but I am not Elizabeth's mother."

"We both know that I am not his father, but I'm willing to accept him as my son if you will accept Elizabeth. We will adopt her as a war orphan and a new birth certificate will be issued. No one will think it strange. According to Sam, people believe that you simply stayed in Charleston while I was overseas because you were devastated when Michael's visit to see me, his father, ended in the bombing of our London home. That you believed that both of us were dead until Minette found him and brought him home, along with Elizabeth. It is the story of a miracle, and people love a miracle with a happy ending."

"But they were here for months before I came back."

"Honestly, Sylvia, do you really think anyone will question you if you allude to the terrible shock you suffered and how happy you are to have your family back together again. Just don't give them details and gossip will die down quickly, if there is any gossip at all."

"Why, John? Why not just divorce me and take Elizabeth?"

"Because she loves Michael, and I want her to be happy. It's as simple as that. I know we don't love each other and that our marriage is over, but people live in loveless marriages all the time and for many reasons, and I think giving two children happiness, security, and love is a good reason. It will protect your inheritance and it will protect both children."

Sylvia sat silently considering his proposal. John watched as a variety of emotions chased across her face. Finally she said, "What about Valerie? Michael knows about her. He actually thinks he talks to her."

"I'm sure he'll outgrow that, it's just his imagination." He heard himself repeat Sam's words. "If we explain adoption to them both, they'll know that we, you and I, are their parents."

"John," she said seriously, "I'm not sure I can be a mother to Elizabeth. If you remember, I'm not even a good mother to Michael. Minette has been taking care of all that. Some days, I don't even see them. I don't like being a mother any more than my mother wanted to be with me."

"Oh, Syl, I know this has been very hard for you. Now that the war is over, we'll be able to hire help again, and the children are in school most of the year. I think we can do this. I blamed you for my unhappiness, and I was very angry when Michael was born, but I've had time to think about what I want from life. I know that falling in love with Valerie was no different than you falling in love with Michael's father. If I could, I'd agree to a divorce, but we've tried to break the will and it just isn't possible. So, for now, please, let's adopt Elizabeth and show a brave, united face to the world."

"You're very persuasive, John. I understand what is in it for the children and what you get for yourself, but why would I tie myself to a man who admits that he doesn't love me and that he doesn't want to live as man and wife?"

"Protection. Plain and simple. No matter what you do, no matter how you live your life, if you keep the secret of Elizabeth's birth, I will keep the secret of Michael's. You are free to be exactly who you are. You don't need to interact with the children any more than is comfortable for you."

The next morning, they reached the decision that Valerie would never be mentioned as more than a person that John knew in England, a pregnant woman whose husband was killed in the war, a person that he had befriended, a lovely friend who had been willing to take in his son and nanny when they visited London, a woman who had given birth to Elizabeth and then died in a bomb explosion. That Elizabeth was an orphan that the nanny had saved, along with Michael, on the night of the bombing and then placed in the care of her parents in Wales. The story they would tell together would concentrate on the bravery of the nanny and the miraculous way that Minette had discovered them and brought them home. And always they would mention how happy they were to be able to adopt Elizabeth and make her a part of their family.

The City Chronicle
May 14, 1948

Tattletales by Sharon Chatsworth

Celebration plans are in the air at the John Augustus home. The war orphan, brought to the States by Mrs. Minette Augustus, will soon be an official member of the family. What a lucky little girl! But… perhaps there is even more reason to celebrate. I've heard from a very good source that a certain Englishman will be visiting for the party. Are there wedding bells in the air?

Chapter Twelve

With the war ended, the world seemed to change at a rapid pace. The soldiers came home and found peacetime jobs in industries that were turning from producing war equipment to creating consumer goods. The American economy was stronger than ever. The G.I. Bill made it possible for veterans to buy houses and go back to school. It seemed like everyone was pregnant.

Sylvia attended yet another baby shower and smiled at the ribbing of her friends. "Two are quite enough," she declared. No one knew that she and John were living separate lives. They seldom interacted in the house, but in public they appeared to be a stable couple. It wasn't as difficult to fool her friends as Sylvia had expected. Most people didn't even ask questions, at least now that people were getting back into the normal whirl of social activities and there were parties and galas to attend. Elizabeth's adoption would be final soon, and John had insisted that they have a party of their own to celebrate. It would be fun to hostess a party even if it was for *that* child.

The new-mother's helper—Sylvia thought that a silly name for a nanny—could take the children away after a decent interval, and the adults would be able to enjoy themselves. Of course, the family would all be in attendance and that meant it wouldn't be as much fun. She lit a cigarette and turned her attention back to the mother-to-be.

Minette opened the newest letter from Henry as she drank her morning coffee. She missed seeing the children at breakfast each morning, but she did see them often, in fact, almost every day. Sylvia had made it quite clear that she wasn't interested in school events or projects, so Minette continued to attend the events and help with the children's projects. They often came to her home directly after school. She was so proud of the two of them.

Elizabeth was blooming in her first year at St. Agatha's Academy. She was reading and writing well above grade level mostly, Minette thought, due to Michael's patient tutoring. They were still inseparable, even though Sylvia had insisted that they move into individual bedrooms. Most nights, Michael was still the one who read a story to Elizabeth and waited until she fell asleep.

Minette brought her attention back to the letter. Her friendship with Henry had grown into something more. She wasn't sure she could call it love, they'd spent so little time actually together, but she'd invited him to visit. She smiled broadly as she realized that not only was he accepting her invitation, he was planning his trip now and would be in the city for Elizabeth's adoption party. He said he felt like Elizabeth was his granddaughter, "What with being there when she was found." She quickly wrote a note back and hurried to the post box to send it on its way. She felt like skipping!

Helen struggled to load Sarah's wheelchair into the car. It was the latest indicator that Sarah's heart was continuing to deteriorate, but no way was Helen leaving her out of the fun of shopping for party dresses to wear to Elizabeth's adoption party. They planned to swing by St. Agatha's and pick up Jennifer and Beth and then the four of them would go downtown to have tea at Bergdorf and shop for new outfits. It might be extravagant to buy clothing Sarah didn't really need, but Helen wanted to make as many happy memories for her as possible.

The girls were full of chatter and school news. Helen half listened as she watched her two older daughters devour the finger sandwiches and fairy cakes. Sarah's face glowed, and she laughed at their stories as she nibbled at a cake. They were all growing up so fast.

Christopher would graduate from college in June. He'd followed his dream and was joining the newly formed United States Air Force with the hope of becoming a pilot. Peter was a college sophomore now, and she and Sam were hopeful that he was settling down and would follow his father into the law. If the ability to argue his case were any indicator of a talent for the law, Peter certainly had the talent. Jennifer would graduate from high school in June and so far had made no decisions about the future. She was a beautiful, popular girl. The young men swarmed around her but she'd given no indication that any one was of more interest than any other. Helen thought she might choose secretarial school instead of college. Beth, on the other hand, just graduating from grammar school, knew exactly what she wanted, a degree from Radcliffe, and then she planned to become a rich and famous editor for *Vogue* magazine, and Helen and Sam had no doubt that she would manage to get what she wanted. Nothing could stand up to a siege from Beth.

Sarah, too, had dreams of the future, but at nine her dreams tended toward catching a fairy in the garden. She seldom spoke of attending "real school" any more, but Helen knew that she wanted that more than anything. "So," Helen said, stopping her woolgathering and standing up, "let's go shopping."

After discussing the adoption party with Sylvia, John had turned to Minette and Mrs. Peters and requested that they make it child friendly. Sylvia would handle the adult portion of the party, but this was to be a celebration of Elizabeth becoming a full member of the family and he wanted her to always remember how much she was wanted and loved. He knew that Sylvia was finding it impossible to feel like a mother to Elizabeth, but he recalled how he had felt when he realized that Michael could not be his natural son and he hoped that her feelings would change the way his had changed toward Michael. If he was honest with himself, he knew that he didn't love him the way he did Elizabeth, but he did enjoy knowing him and he no longer was angry when someone called him his son. Perhaps they could become a family after all.

By Friday night, Elizabeth was beside herself with excitement. She twirled around her room, her full skirts flying out and her arms raised high. "You're my real brother now, Michael, and John is my real father. The judge said so."

"I am. But you better calm down. We have to go downstairs and greet the guests, and you don't want mother to be angry. Come here and let me straighten your dress."

Elizabeth acquiesced, and they headed down the wide front stairway, hand in hand. John looked up and caught sight of them first. He smiled broadly and called out, "Welcome to the Augustus family." Elizabeth grinned back and giggled. Michael smiled and let go so she could run down and jump into John's open arms. Sylvia gulped the remainder of her drink and joined them at the bottom of the stairs.

Elizabeth stood between her parents, greeting each guest as she'd been taught. She glanced often toward Michael and he gave her the thumbs up sign each time. No one but Michael seemed to notice that Sylvia didn't touch the girl. Michael found it strange that his mother would want to adopt Elizabeth when she didn't seem to like her or want her around.

Michael caught his uncle watching him, and he went over to stand with him while his parents and Elizabeth finished welcoming the guests. "Christopher is around here somewhere," Sam said. "Why don't you go find him?"

"I'll wait for Elizabeth. She might need me."

Sam nodded.

It wasn't long before the guests were settled, the congratulations said, and the children released to the yard for games and refreshments. Jennifer stayed behind with the adults and Christopher and Peter joined the younger children. They sprawled across the stairs and soon Michael joined them. Peter grinned at him. "Now that you have a sister, you'll soon find out what a pain they can be." Michael smiled back, but he didn't believe that Elizabeth would ever be a pain.

The party was a huge success. It was the first party the Augustus family had hosted since the war, and everyone had accepted the invitation. The women were delighted to be wearing cocktail dresses and they buzzed about, discussing dresses, shoes, and children. The men, also glad to be wearing something other than uniforms, talked about the booming economy and the political and military tensions outlined in Walter Lippmann's new book, *Cold War*.

People crowded around Minette and Henry, and they repeated the story of finding Michael and Elizabeth in Wales numerous times. When asked, Sylvia added to the story only how frightened she had been during the time that Michael was missing.

As the evening came to a close, Christopher found himself alone with Michael. "I need to ask you something, Michael." His urgency was apparent, and they stopped together in the shadows. "Do you still hear from Elizabeth's mother?"

Michael hesitated. He never talked about Valerie any more, but something in Chris' tone caused him to say, "Yes, why?"

"Sarah is very sick." Michael nodded and Chris hurried on. "Do you think she could help?"

"I don't think it works that way. She mostly just watches out for Elizabeth and tells me to take care of stuff." He saw Chris' disappointment. "But I can ask her... I like Sarah, too, and if we could help her that would be terrific." He took a deep breath. "Valerie isn't here right now. But I promise I'll try."

Before going up to bed, Elizabeth hugged John and said, "Thank you for adopting me, Dad!" She turned toward Sylvia to hug her, too, but Sylvia's back was turned and she was walking away. John didn't notice Elizabeth's disappointment, he was simply too thrilled to be called *Dad* by his daughter.

The City Chronicle
April 15, 1949

Tattletales by Sharon Chatsworth

I learned today that Mr. Christopher Augustus, son of Samuel and Helen Augustus, is home on leave for a few days. He is currently flying with the boys of the United States Air Force as they participate in the Berlin Airlift. Our brave young men, along with aircrews from the United Kingdom, Canada, Australia, New Zealand, and South Africa, have flown over 200,000 flights and provided 4,700 tons of daily necessities, such as fuel and food, to the Berliners.

Chapter Thirteen

"For heaven's sake, Michael, what is wrong with you?" Sylvia glared at her son. "I thought we'd gotten past all this foolishness. You're almost twelve years old. You shouldn't be talking to your imaginary friends."

Michael knew better than to protest. Sylvia had never been a warm, loving mother and when she was angry he was never sure what might happen. He wondered what she knew. "It's bad enough that the family knows how crazy you are, but when I hear about it from my friends what am I supposed to say?" She caught sight of Elizabeth in the hall and continued, "And you, you're no better than he is. We give you a lovely home and what thanks do we get? You babble on about your 'real' mother. It's disgusting! Go away, both of you."

Sylvia paced the living room waiting for John to arrive. She was tired of living like this, and it was time that John stepped up and fixed things. Elizabeth was always underfoot and now Michael was talking about that damn ghost again. She wanted a drink... Just one to take the edge off, but as she started to pour she heard the front door open. She set the crystal decanter down and turned away from the bar. "John," she called, "please come in."

"Where are the kids?" John asked, setting his briefcase down and flopping into a chair.

"Hiding from me, I imagine. You have to do something about them." Like the children, John had learned to proceed cautiously when Sylvia was in one of her moods. He cocked an eyebrow and waited. "At lunch today, that damn Angela Carter was regaling everyone with stories about Elizabeth. Her son is in the same class, and it seems your darling little Elizabeth has told everyone that Michael talks to her 'real' mother." John sat up. "I thought that was over, John. You promised that Michael would outgrow it. It has to stop. People will think he's crazy or that Elizabeth is and you know you don't want that to happen."

"They are children, Syl. No one pays any attention to them. If we ignore it, so will others."

"Don't be an idiot, John. When Elizabeth tells her friends that her big brother talks to the ghost of her mother, there are only two possible conclusions—one, that Elizabeth is crazy, or two, that Michael is crazy. Either way, one of your children is crazy, and therefore I am not a good mother and I won't allow people to say that I am not a good mother!"

John almost smiled at the way Sylvia had managed to twist her complaint and make it about herself. He wasn't surprised; he knew that the only thing that really mattered to Sylvia was what others thought of her. "I'll talk to our"—he emphasized the *our*—"children tonight. Michael knows that talking about Valerie upsets you. If Elizabeth is talking about it, something must have happened."

Finding the children in the kitchen, John settled himself next to Michael and chatted about school and friends before asking, "Michael, your mother tells me you've been talking to Valerie." Michael hung his head. "It's all right, son. I just want to know what is going on. You know that some people become very upset when you talk about her."

"I know, Papa, and I try not to talk to her, but when Christopher was home on leave last week, he asked me to ask her if Sarah was going to get well, and I had to do that because I wanted to know, too. And then Elizabeth caught me talking and she wanted me to ask what she should do to make Sylvia like her, and I guess Elizabeth must have told her friends what Valerie said, even though I told her not to." Michael grabbed a breath and plunged on. "I told her not to tell anyone, Dad. I really did."

"I'm sure you did, Michael." He knew he shouldn't ask, but he couldn't stop himself. "Do you still talk to Valerie a lot?"

"Not so much, but when I have a question she's always there. I know other people think it's crazy so I don't talk about it, but Christopher already knows and he's really worried about Sarah."

John nodded. "So what did she tell you?"

"It's sad." John nodded again. "She said that Sarah is really sick and that unless the doctors can help her soon it may be too late. She told me to tell Chris to have his parents look for doctors trying new procedures. I didn't really know what that meant, but Chris said that he'd help them look. Then Elizabeth came in and I asked Valerie her questions and she just shook her head and told me to tell Elizabeth that you, Dad, loved her very much and that if she was a good girl and studied hard everything would be okay."

"Thank you, Michael. You didn't do anything wrong, but your mother is quite upset, so it would be good to keep conversations with Valerie to yourself. I'll talk to Elizabeth. You go along and get your homework done." John sat staring at the empty fireplace. He'd give anything to see or hear Valerie one more time. He missed her every day. If only they could raise Elizabeth together. He wasn't sure what he would say, but he needed to assure Elizabeth that it wasn't her fault that Sylvia acted the way she did.

At the annual May Day Luncheon, Sylvia told her friends that she was leaving for Charleston to take care of family business and that it would most likely take a long time, at least all summer. That evening, she informed the family that she was going "back home" to Charleston and that "if it was necessary" the children could visit her there over the summer holiday. Privately, she told John that she would not be returning. Minette, upon hearing the news, wrote to Henry saying that while it was not a surprise it was sad that the children seemed relieved by their mother's departure.

John explained carefully to them that it wasn't their fault that Sylvia was living in her other house, but he needn't have worried. Instead of being sad, the children seemed to blossom and the house rang with both their noise and the noise of their friends. It was, John admitted to himself, as if a terrible burden had been lifted from them all.

As summer approached, they made plans to spend time at Sam's house in the country and visits to Sylvia were never mentioned.

The City Chronicle
January 4, 1950

Tattletales by Sharon Chatsworth

Cupid has been busy early this year! John Augustus has announced the pending nuptials of his mother, Mrs. Minette Rothchild Augustus, to Mr. Henry Smyth of London, England. The small family wedding will be held in the chapel of Trinity School on February 14.

Chapter Fourteen

It was never good news when Sylvia called John at the office, so when his secretary announced the call, he motioned for her to close the door before he picked up the telephone. Without bothering to respond to his greeting, Sylvia burst into a tirade about how embarrassing it was that his "old mother" was getting married and not only *married* but married in a *church*. "What is she thinking?" Sylvia demanded.

"I imagine she is thinking about how happy she is and how much she wants to share the rest of her life with Henry."

"She's seventy-two, John! How much life can she possibly have left?" She caught herself. "I didn't exactly mean that, but you must see that it's embarrassing."

"You already said that, Syl, and I have to tell you I never find Minette embarrassing, but I find your call both annoying and embarrassing. Did you call just to say you don't approve of my mother marrying the man she loves?"

"I called to tell you I don't want my son exposed to any more of this. I've enrolled him as a boarding student at Trinity next semester."

"You've what? You can't do that without discussing it with me."

"I can and I have. He is *my* son, as you have so often told me, and I've heard from numerous friends that he is still too entangled with Elizabeth and that damn ghost. He needs a dose of reality before it's too late."

"But—"

"But nothing. You and your crazy mother encourage his imagination. He needs to grow up. I've thought this over very carefully and the arrangements are complete. When school begins again on Monday, he will begin as a boarding student. You will need to explain it to him and move him into his room before then. The arrangements have all been made. You should get a letter today with his room assignment and a list of everything he needs to bring."

"Wait a minute. You haven't told him? You didn't ask him if he wanted to do this? What's wrong with you, Syl?"

"Nothing is wrong with me, John. I'm simply doing what I feel is best for my son. He obviously needs a change in attitude. I invited him here for Christmas, and he didn't even bother to give me a civil refusal."

Crap! John thought. So that was it. Michael hadn't mentioned an invitation. "Syl, I'm sure that must have been a misunderstanding. Perhaps he never received your invitation."

"He received it all right. I spoke to him on the phone, and when he said you already had plans for the holiday I asked him to think it over and let me know. I want him to learn better manners and to focus on his studies. Certainly, you can understand that? After all, appearances have always been very important to your family."

John knew that Michael didn't seem to miss his mother and that he had wanted to spend Christmas with Elizabeth and his cousins. With Sylvia living in Charleston, they almost never spoke or even thought about her.

It sounded like that oversight had hurt her feelings or, more likely, he admitted to himself, someone had asked why she wasn't sharing the holidays with her husband and children and she'd been embarrassed. Now, in her usual charming manner, she was overreacting and Michael would pay.

He put off talking to Michael as long as possible, but after Elizabeth was settled for the night he knocked on Michael's door and entered. The boy looked up from his homework and smiled. John knew he'd come to like this child a great deal. Perhaps he didn't fully love him as he would a son of his own, but he was a great kid and John was proud to call him his son. There was no way to make his message easier. He told him straight and simple what was happening.

Michael's face registered the shock of those words. "Monday. This Monday? Is that even possible?"

"I'm afraid it is. Your mother made all the arrangements and I received a confirmation letter today. She really thinks it is best that you board at Trinity." Michael turned away and then sat perfectly still. John reached out to touch his shoulder but stopped his hand in midair. "I tried to talk your mother out of this, but she is determined."

"Can't you just say no?" Michael turned and looked at John his eyes pleading, and John had to turn away. "You're my father. Just tell her you want me to stay with Elizabeth, to live at home."

"I can't, Michael. I really wish I could, but you need to do this. You'll be able to come home every weekend if you want and even sometimes during the week. I know it's not the same, but your mother insists and the arrangements have all been made. We need to tell Elizabeth in the morning. I'm sorry."

Michael nodded but refused to look at John, and, after a long moment, John left the room.

At breakfast, Elizabeth's reaction was much worse than anything John could have imagined. On hearing the news that Michael would be going to live at his school, she burst into dramatic sobs and demanded that he fix this. When he said he couldn't, she stomped out of the room, declaring that a "real daddy" would have fixed it.

John wanted to scream out his innocence in this ridiculous dilemma, but Elizabeth was right. Even if she didn't know that he was her "real daddy" and not Michael's, he should be able to fix it.

He called Sylvia again and pleaded that she change her mind and allow Michael to continue to live at home. He only succeeded in making her angrier when he mentioned Elizabeth's reaction to Michael going away. Instead of relenting, Sylvia threatened that if

Michael didn't become a boarding student, she would remove him from Trinity School and enroll him far enough away that he wouldn't be able to get home until summer.

Even her grandmother's wedding plans and her beautiful new dress couldn't lift Elizabeth's spirits. She was heartbroken. Each afternoon she went straight to her room and wrote a letter to Michael begging that he come home and live with her. Michael wrote back explaining again that he was only a few miles away and telling her that he would be home again each Saturday.

But the short weekends were too short. Elizabeth hung onto Michael, never leaving his side from the moment he arrived on Saturday morning until he had to leave again on Sunday afternoon. Each weekend, Elizabeth seemed to sob harder as she hugged him good-bye.

John avoided catching Michael's eye. He was ashamed that he couldn't stand up to Sylvia and demand that Michael be allowed to live at home. Even Minette, who tried to stay out of family situations, counseled John that it wasn't right to see the children suffering this way.

John requested that Michael be allowed to live at home the week of Minette's wedding, so that he could participate in all the festivities. It was a good idea. Elizabeth was buzzing with happiness. As the rehearsal dinner unfolded, he kept an eye on the two of them as they laughed and talked with their cousins. He knew that that Chatsworth woman would probably report on the absence of Sylvia at this family occasion, but, he admitted to himself, it was much nicer that she wasn't present. He raised his glass in a toast. "To my mother. May you know nothing but happiness from this day forward. I love you."

Elizabeth watched the adults and then she stood up and raised her glass. "I want to toast, too." The guests smiled indulgently. "To Grandmother and Grandpa Henry. Thank you for finding me and bringing me and Michael to America. Now please bring Michael home."

For a moment there was silence and then Henry clinked his glass with Minette's and said gravely, "You're very welcome, sweetheart. I promise to see what I can do."

John knew that both his mother and Henry thought it was wrong to separate the children. Sam agreed and so did Helen. It was time that he stood up to Sylvia before they did more damage to these two wonderful children. He called the school and requested that Michael be changed back to day-student status. Mr. Phillips, Head of Trinity School, accepted the request and agreed that the change could take place at once. He knew that he had an obligation to inform Mrs. Augustus that her son was no longer a boarding student, but he felt he could wait until asked. After all, it was Mr. Augustus who paid the bills and attended school events.

The City Chronicle
April 8, 1950

Tattletales by Sharon Chatsworth

It's a prosperous time in America. Many of our brave young men have earned financial independence through education provided by the G.I. Bill and are now able to buy homes of their own. Families are growing and mothers are able to stay home and care for their children and homes. This newspaper supports family values and is proud to announce that, beginning tomorrow, an entire section of our fine Sunday edition will be devoted to the moral and ethical principles traditionally upheld and transmitted within a family, morals such as honesty, loyalty, industry, and faith. We will provide home-making tips, healthy and economical recipe and menu ideas, fashionable sewing patterns, craft ideas, and more to encourage American woman to raise moral American citizens.

Chapter Fifteen

With Michael back at home and Sylvia living in Charleston, life seemed almost perfect. John dreaded what would happen when Sylvia found out about Michael, but he was willing to stand firm for once. Elizabeth's happiness was the most important thing in his life. Between the Cold War and the growing threat of war in Korea, AmCo continued to grow. Minette and Henry were still in England on a prolonged honeymoon. Summer would be here soon, and the kids had a million plans. John and Sam had discussed John buying a summer place near Sam and Helen, so when Sam asked for a few minutes of time, John felt no apprehension, but one look at Sam's face changed that.

"I've been on the phone with Mr. Patterson," he said, sinking into a chair and propping his feet on the coffee table.

"From Alex's attorney in Charleston? Is he still alive?"

"He's alive and well and still looking out for Alexander's interests."

"Sylvia's father was a brilliant businessman. It's not surprising that he chose an excellent law firm to represent him. Is there something happening with his estate?" For a moment, the thought of a divorce from Sylvia flitted across John's mind, but it didn't really matter anymore, although he supposed it would make Sylvia happy.

"Yes and no." Sam paused, choosing his words carefully. "A murder charge against Sylvia for the accident in 1940 is being considered." John started to protest. Sam stopped him with a wave of his hand. "There is no statute of limitations on murder. If Sylvia hadn't been admitted to the hospital for psychiatric care so quickly, a murder charge might have been made at the time of the deaths."

"It was an accident."

Sam refused to excuse Sylvia. "We all know she was drinking, and even though there is no law in South Carolina that prohibits drinking and driving, five people died that afternoon, and now the police have let Mr. Patterson know that someone has brought it back to the attention of the district attorney." Sam began to pace and the two men considered what this news meant to the family and to Sylvia.

"Could she go to prison?"

"I suppose, but I don't think that's what anyone wants. If it were, I don't think Mr. Patterson would have been alerted to the pending charges. I think someone wants something else, perhaps money, perhaps an apology. I really can't guess. Mr. Patterson called me as AmCo's attorney. He is going to speak to the district attorney and then to Sylvia. After that, he'll be in touch with me. I just wanted to keep you informed. We need to be prepared if this goes further." John stood, but again Sam waved him to silence. "If Sylvia is charged with anything, even involuntary manslaughter, it will affect the entire family and the corporation."

"Walter must be rolling over in his grave."

"This is no worse than other scandals this family has hidden. I never thought I'd say it, but I think Grandfather was right. Family matters belong in the family. No one else needs to know anything. We'll handle this, Cuz."

"I think this might be the biggest scandal of them all if it gets out," John said. Sam didn't reply. He thought of the birth and murder of John's father and the subsequent lies that had been handling that situation for almost forty years. John continued, "But I'll follow your lead. You're the lawyer. What do you want me to do?"

"Mr. Patterson suggested, and I agreed, that he should handle the initial approach to both the state of South Carolina and Sylvia, and so right now we wait. He knows the local people and he'll be able to determine why this is surfacing now."

It only took three days before Sam reported that he'd spoken to Mr. Patterson again. He'd been able to determine that Beau Campbell's brother, Jeb, was the one seeking a charge against Sylvia. Patterson had learned that Jeb Campbell was considering a run for the governorship of South Carolina in 1954 and was looking to build his name recognition by pushing for retribution for the families of the children killed in the crash.

"Patterson thinks that Campbell's belief is that a murder charge would bring him the publicity that he wants. He will appear to champion black children, the Southern Baptist Church, his own widowed sister-in-law and speak out against drunk driving all at the same time."

"So, what do we do, Sam? How can we stop this? I'd like to see Sylvia pay for her actions, but I don't want to harm the children or the family."

"Mr. Patterson thinks that if Sylvia were to leave Charleston, the talk would die down and," - he paused, - "if AmCo were to make a sizeable contribution to the Campbell campaign it would certainly help."

John nodded. "Has he spoken to Sylvia?"

"Yes. She's thinking it over. He was very polite, but I gathered that Sylvia wasn't happy that she'd need to move back to the city."

John brushed his hair back from his forehead. "None of us will be happy if she decides to move back here."

"I think we need to consider the contribution. After all, Charleston is a major port, and we'd support someone in the gubernatorial race anyway. Mr. Patterson suggests that $20,000 would be appropriate."

"Isn't that more than the campaign will cost?"

"Probably, but I don't think this is really about campaign costs, do you?"

"No, I suppose not, but it seems like a payoff." Sam stayed quiet, letting John think about the consequences. "How long do you think we have before the papers get hold of this?"

"Mr. Patterson suggests that we move quickly. I think you need to talk to Sylvia immediately and make arrangements for her to leave Charleston."

John knew he should call Sylvia at once, but he dreaded the call. He was fairly certain that she was drinking again, and he told himself that the next morning would be a better time. He'd managed to put the call completely out of his mind, so when the phone rang during dinner he thought nothing of it as Michael jumped up to answer. But when he returned to the table and said, "It's Mother. She'd like to talk to you." John knew it wasn't good.

"Sylvia," he said, making his voice intentionally calm. "I was planning on calling you in the morning."

"And when were you planning to tell me that Michael, my son, Michael, is no longer a boarding student at Trinity?"

"They were both so unhappy that I decided to allow Michael to return to being a day student."

"*They*? Or your darling Elizabeth? I told you I didn't want him spending so much time with her."

"And I decided that your request was ridiculous. He's my son, too. And I want him to live at home."

"You do know that I would only need to make one phone call to that Chatsworth woman and everyone in the city would know that Elizabeth is your illegitimate daughter?"

"Don't threaten me, Sylvia. Do you really want to start an ugly, scandalous, name-calling argument? What will your friends think when they discover that Michael is not my child? If you don't leave this alone, I'll take Elizabeth and divorce you. Your father's will is still in effect, and you won't like living with no money and no friends." John glanced toward the kitchen. The door was open, but he was sure the children couldn't hear their conversation. "Don't you have enough worries right now without starting another fight with me? Michael and Elizabeth are both doing well in school.

They are good, happy kids and you need to leave them alone."

"Actually," Sylvia almost purred. John was amazed at her quick change of tone. "I was calling to talk to you about that. I really think I need to go to Paris for a few months. With the war and all, I haven't been over in years and this seems like a good time. I've booked passage on RMS *Queen Elizabeth* next week. I'll come up this Friday and say good-bye to you and the children." She paused, and when John didn't say anything, she continued. "I'll need a bigger allowance, darling. It's very expensive in Paris now, and I really do think I should get an apartment."

John knew a bargain when he heard one. With Sylvia in Paris with money to spend, she'd go back to ignoring the children and their living arrangements. "Have you discussed this with Mr. Patterson?" he asked cautiously.

"He's such an old fuddy-duddy. He tried to scare me with some silly lawsuit about that dumb accident, but when I told him I was thinking of living in Paris for a few years, he agreed that that seemed like a good idea."

John noticed that her "few months in Paris" had changed to "a few years," but he didn't call her out on it. If she was in Europe, she wouldn't be interfering in their lives and people would soon stop wondering where she was and what she was doing.

Sam provided a check to Mr. Patterson for the Campbell campaign and John set up a generous line of credit for Sylvia in France. Her brief visit went smoothly and quickly and neither of the children seemed concerned that their mother would not be living in the United States.

Minette and Henry spent as much time as possible with the children and noticed that Sylvia's departure didn't create so much as a ruffle. They agreed that her departure was for the best and were delighted to spend time with the children.

Life settled into a routine. Work, school, and family, it was all good. Elizabeth grew to look more like Valerie every day, and John delighted in being her father. He regretted the loss of the love of his life and was actually glad that friends, knowing he and Sylvia were married, didn't try to set him up on dates.

Sam and Helen were happy for John and the children and often spent evenings and weekends with them at one house or the other. Their children were growing up so fast. Sarah's poor health was always a concern, but Jennifer was engaged to be married and Sarah was thrilled to be a bridesmaid and determined that she would walk down the aisle instead of using her wheelchair. Jennifer assured her that she would be a beautiful bridesmaid and that the chair would be decorated with flowers and it would be perfect.

Helen watched her daughters together as they planned, and she realized how lucky they were to have raised such wonderful children. Peter would take the bar exam this year with the intention of joining his father in practice. Christopher, of course, wasn't home much. The Air Force kept him busy, but she knew that he loved what he was doing, and she prayed for his safety and that another war would not develop in Korea.

The City Chronicle
June 21, 1952

Tattletales by Sharon Chatsworth

Jennifer Augustus was a beautiful, blushing bride this afternoon as her father, Samuel Augustus, gave her hand in marriage to Geoff Fulbright, head of the esteemed Fulbright bank. While everyone knows money marries money, this appears to be a true love match. The couple met at a party two years ago and have had eyes only for each other since that first glance.

Chapter Sixteen

Jennifer was gorgeous in her New Look wedding gown. The creamy-white satin accentuated her glowing skin and the below-mid-calf full skirted, pointed bustline, small waist, and rounded shoulder line of this radical new silhouette seemed to have been created just for her. Sam smiled proudly as Jennifer took his arm to walk down the aisle.

The crowd stood as they passed. Sam caught Helen's eye and smiled at her tears. They were delighted with Jennifer's choice of husband. Geoff was older and established in business and quite obviously adored their daughter. The engagement had lasted two years, and at times they wondered if there would be a wedding, but today everything was perfect.

Sam said his line, placed his daughter's hand in Geoff's, and returned to the pew to sit next to his wife. If only Sarah were healthy, life would be completely good. They were a fortunate family. Christopher, resplendent in his dress uniform, stood next to the groom, sober and unsmiling, intent on performing his duties as the best man. Sam supposed he'd be the next to marry, or, he caught himself, more likely Peter would be next. Christopher was so busy with his career that he didn't seem to have time to fall in love, while Peter fell in love every month and, sooner or later, one of his young ladies would hold his interest for more than a month or two.

The music swelled and Sam's attention returned to the ceremony. Jennifer and Geoff smiled triumphantly as they strode up the aisle. Christopher offered his arm to his sister Beth. Peter swung Sarah's wheelchair around and the four of them followed the bride and groom.

Late that night, back at home, Sarah snuggled close to Sam. "Daddy," she said, "I'm really tired, but it was so much fun to be Jen's bridesmaid. Wasn't she beautiful?"

"She was, and so are you. I have the most beautiful daughters in the world."

Sarah grinned and then sobered. "Do you think I'll ever get married?"

"Of course, you will. You're only thirteen. Soon the boys will be swarming around here, asking for your hand in marriage.

But now it's time for bed. You know your mother and I don't let you girls date until you are sixteen. You've got plenty of time."

"Daddy"—Sarah kept her eyes on her hands—"I really want to have a boyfriend before I die."

"Oh, sweetie, you'll have a dozen boyfriends." He kissed the curls on the top of her head, afraid to catch her eye for fear that she would see the tears in his. "Now head for bed. It's been a long day, and you need your beauty rest if you are going to start chasing boys."

Sarah giggled and kissed him good night. Sam poured himself a nightcap and sat staring into the distance. He would give every material thing he had if he could make Sarah's heart strong.

Over the summer, the family watched Sarah lose more of her energy. She never seemed to complain, but she spent more of her time sleeping and seldom had the energy to be up and about. Beth was busy and excited, getting ready for her first year at Radcliffe. She'd found a list in *Mademoiselle* titled "Clothing for the Well-dressed Freshman" and had received the needs list from college. Sam and Helen laughed at her excitement but they encouraged her to find everything on the lists. Beth showed Sarah every purchase and gathered her opinion on every outfit. Sarah kept track of the packing lists, carefully checking off each item. Geoff often dropped Jennifer off at the house on his way to the city in the morning, so that she could spend the day and join in the discussions about sweater sets, pearls, hats, and gloves. Chris and Peter were seldom home, but when they were they, too, made time to spend with Sarah. It was obvious, although it was never discussed, that everyone in the family was concerned about Sarah's declining health.

Helen searched publications for any advances in medicine. Johns Hopkins Hospital was having continuing success operating on "blue babies" and correcting congenital heart defects. Helen had taken Sarah to Baltimore in 1950, but the doctors there had not felt they could operate successfully. The hole in Sarah's heart was too large, the risk too great. It broke her heart to watch Sarah's failing health, and she lived in fear that she would lose her youngest daughter.

Michael and Elizabeth often spent time with their cousins. One afternoon, while Michael and Sarah sprawled on the wide front porch playing Monopoly and chatting about what would happen when school started in the fall, Sarah stopped in the middle of shaking the dice cup and said, "Michael I need to talk to Valerie."

"Valerie? Valerie who?"

"You know who. Don't pretend you don't. I have a question that I need answered."

"I was just a kid when I believed in Valerie. She was my imaginary friend."

"No, she wasn't." Sarah stared at him sternly. "I know your mother said that, but it wasn't true, and it isn't true now. You need to tell her I have a question."

"Sarah, it doesn't work that way." Michael shook his head. "I can't just call her on the phone."

"But you do still see her and talk to her, don't you?"

Michael looked around, and, seeing Elizabeth playing badminton on the lawn with Beth, he lowered his voice and answered, "Sometimes. I think she kind of watches out for Elizabeth, and when something is wrong she tells me. But I don't like anyone to know. They'd think I was crazy."

"Well, I don't think you're crazy. I think you are very smart, and I need Valerie to tell me if I'm going to die." Sarah's eyes shone out of her thin face and her urgency was apparent. Michael reached across the board and touched her hand.

"Are you afraid?" he asked. Sarah nodded. "I'll try, Sarah, but I don't know if I'll see her."

Sarah shook the dice again and rolled them across the board. "Thank you."

When he'd been younger, it seemed like Valerie was always there, but after Sylvia moved to Paris, he seldom even felt her presence. Now, as much as he wanted to help Sarah, he had no idea how or if he could contact Valerie. "Let's finish later, Sarah. I'm going to take a walk." He jumped off the porch and, avoiding the rest of the family, he headed toward the lake.

He felt nothing except sadness. Sarah was so sweet, and while she'd always been sick, he'd never thought about her actually dying before. It didn't seem right that a kid could die. He picked up a stick and swished it through the long grass as he walked. It was hot and quiet here by himself. He found a large flat rock and sat on it, gazing out at the water and wishing he'd see Valerie but nothing happened. After a while, he walked back to the house, got lemonade from the kitchen, and lay down in the hammock where he drifted off to sleep.

Starting awake at the sound of his name, at first he thought it was Valerie, but then he recognized Beth calling him to dinner. Sarah caught his eye as he took his place at the table, but he shook his head, and she dropped her eyes to her plate. "What are you two up to?" Elizabeth asked, catching their exchange.

"Nothing," they said together, and everyone laughed.

Days went by and Michael tried to concentrate on seeing Valerie but he had no luck conjuring her presence, and the long days of summer drew to a close. Michael and Elizabeth returned to the city, and Beth went off to college, moving into her private room in Moors Hall and declaring that she would soon be a graduate of the Radcliffe Publishing Course and a leader in the publishing world. Sam and Helen chuckled at their middle daughter's enthusiasm and encouraged her to concentrate on one year at a time, enjoy herself, and get good grades. But they admitted to each other they had no doubt that if that was what she wanted, she would get it.

Sarah spent an increasing amount of time in her room and was often asleep when anyone peeked in. But each day she asked if Michael had called and Helen finally took it upon herself to call John. "I don't want to be a bother, John, but Sarah asks for Michael every day, and I thought perhaps you could come out for the weekend. It might cheer her up."

John didn't hesitate. He agreed that a fall weekend in the country was just what they needed. He told Michael and Elizabeth that they were going and was surprised by Michael's hesitation. "What's up, son? I thought you'd be thrilled to rake leaves."

"It's not that, Dad. I just don't want to disappoint Sarah." John raised his eyebrows and waited. He'd learned that his children often kept talking if he stayed quiet. "She wants me to do something, and I haven't done it."

"Could I help?"

"I don't think so," Michael said sadly. "You won't be mad if I tell you?"

"Of course not."

"She wants me to ask Valerie something, and I haven't been able to see Valerie or hear her in a long time." John waited. "Sarah wants to know if she is going to die, and I don't know what to tell her." John reached for Michael and, even though he was a teenager, he moved into his father's arms and rested his head on John's shoulder. "Is she going to die, Dad?"

"She's very ill, but I can't answer that. No one can, not even Valerie. Let's go to the country this weekend and have a good time. Perhaps we can cheer Sarah up."

"Whoa, what's going on around here?" John asked as Sam grabbed him in a bear hug and thumped him on the back. "I just saw you a couple of hours ago."

"The Mayo Clinic in Rochester, Minnesota just figured out how to do a heart operation where the patient can survive without their heart beating for ten minutes. They've done it successfully, and they are willing to take a look at Sarah. Helen and I are going to take her to Minnesota as fast as we can."

"Oh, my God!" John hugged Sam in return. "That's the best news I've heard in ages. What can I do to help?"

"Helen has been on the phone all day. The kids are coming home tonight, and we're leaving in the morning. The doctors say she shouldn't fly, so we'll take the train to Chicago and a driver will meet us and take us straight to the Mayo Clinic."

Michael grinned at Sam. "That's great. Where's Sarah? I bet she's excited."

"She's in her room. Go talk to her."

Michael knocked and pushed the door open. Sarah was lying propped up against a pile of pillows. She dropped the book she was pretending to read and beamed. "Did you hear? The doctors are going to fix my heart." Michael nodded and grinned back. Sarah continued, "No wonder Valerie didn't appear, she must have known it would be all right."

Michael wasn't sure that that was the case, but he was thrilled by the news and he simply nodded and agreed. Elizabeth bounced into the room and began to ask a million questions about hospitals and operations, none of which Sarah and Michael could answer. The rest of the family, except Christopher who could not get away, arrived and the evening flew past.

As they boarded the train, Sarah hugged each of her siblings, her cousins, and her Uncle John. There were tears in everyone's eyes, but smiles and excitement reigned as they wished Sarah luck and a quick recovery.

Helen knew it might not be that easy. The doctor had explained that in order to operate on Sarah's heart they would actually cool her body to eighty-one degrees Fahrenheit. At that temperature, she would be able to survive without a pumping heart for ten minutes. During that brief period, the doctors would repair her heart, start it pumping again, and then use a warm water bath to return her body temperature to normal. It was very frightening, and she wasn't sure Sarah really understood what would happen if the doctors agreed to operate, but Helen knew that without the operation it was only a short time before they would lose Sarah, and she was determined to take the risk.

The family waited with bated breath as Sarah was admitted to the Mayo Clinic, was accepted for surgery, and received a surgery date. Sam spoke to each of his children every day, keeping them informed and assuring them that Sarah's spirits were high and that the doctors were hopeful. Chris managed to get leave and joined his parents at the hospital the morning of Sarah's surgery, where he had a moment with Sarah. She smiled sleepily and told him not to worry. He kissed her forehead and said he'd see her in a bit, but he worried. She was so pale and so thin, it didn't seem possible that she could endure what the surgery entailed.

The surgery to repair her heart had to take place in the small window of time her heart would be stopped, but her chest would need to be opened so the heart could be reached and then the chest would be closed. The doctor anticipated that it would take several hours before she would be returned to Intensive Care and perhaps even longer before the family could see her. In any case, they knew she would not be fully awake for a day or more. They huddled together in the family waiting room, sipped at coffee they didn't want, and watched as other families were called from the room.

Finally, it was their turn to follow a nurse down the hall to a smaller room where the doctor waited, his face grim and his eyes serious. "Sarah is a tough little girl," he said.

"She's a real fighter. She is stable, and we are hopeful, but we were only able to partially repair the damage to her heart. It's not an ideal situation. When the heart has had time to stabilize from the shock of the surgery, we will have a much better idea of her prognosis. For now, she is resting, and in a few hours you'll be able to see her." They stared at the doctor unsure of what to say. "I suggest you get some rest. There is nothing you can do here." Sam managed to mutter a thank you, Helen started to cry quietly, and Christopher clenched his jaw and hugged his parents.

The City Chronicle
August 5, 1954

Tattletales by Sharon Chatsworth

It's been a beautiful summer here in our fair city. And nothing has made it brighter than watching the lovely Sarah Augustus blossom into a beautiful young lady. It won't be long before this charmer is breaking hearts and following in her older sisters' footsteps.

Chapter Seventeen

Sarah's recovery had been slow and difficult, but now eighteen months later she was able to enjoy some normal teenage activities. As she dressed for her first real date, Helen bit her lip to avoid cautioning her to be careful. Instead, she straightened the Peter Pan collar on Sarah's crisp white, sleeveless blouse and admired the many rows of colorful rickrack that encircled her bright squaw skirt. Sarah cinched her wide belt around her tiny waist and whirled to give her mother the full view of her outfit. "Do I look right?" she asked anxiously. "Beth said this was what I should wear."

"You look beautiful, darling." Helen hugged her and spun her around again. "You're going to have a wonderful time."

"I hope so, but I don't really know Michael's friend."

Helen smiled. "That's what a date is for, to get to know someone, and double dating with Michael and his girlfriend is the perfect first date."

"Do you think Jeff will know it's my first date?"

"Oh, Sarah." Helen laughed. "Stop worrying. Your cousin would never say or do anything to embarrass you. I'm sure he simply told his house guest that he had a lovely cousin who would be willing to go to the movies. If it wasn't a double date with Michael, we wouldn't allow you to go, you're still only fifteen."

"What if he thinks I'm pathetic?"

"Sarah! Relax! It's just a movie and maybe a bite to eat afterward." She hugged her again. "Now, come on. I hear their voices downstairs."

Despite her fears, Sarah was having a wonderful time. Her date had turned out to be as nice as her mother had predicted. He didn't ask any embarrassing questions about her health, and since her fully buttoned blouse concealed the scar, she was able to believe that maybe he didn't know. She'd been a little embarrassed climbing into the back seat of Michael's car, but Jeff had held the door and then immediately gone around and gotten into the other side, so she hadn't had to wonder how far she should sit from him. On the way to the theater, Michael's girlfriend, Anne, had kept the conversation turned to the new James Stewart movie they were planning to see. *Rear Window* had only been out a couple of days and already people were talking about it and about the beautiful clothes Grace Kelly wore in the movie. "It's a mystery, not a fashion show," Michael teased. Anne had slapped his arm affectionately and said, "You watch the parts you want to watch, and I'll watch the parts I want to watch." They'd laughed, and it had all been much easier than she'd expected. Now, sitting in the dark theater as the lights dimmed and the newsreel started, she smiled happily. This was much better than attending the movies in a wheelchair with her parents.

Sarah watched Michael take Anne's hand as they walked from the movie theater to the soda fountain. She glanced at Jeff and wondered briefly why he didn't take her hand, but he grinned down at her and she relaxed again. As the boys ate cheeseburgers and all four sipped at their lime phosphates, they discussed the movie and Sarah found it easy to banter with the others. Jeff casually draped his arm across the back of the booth, and she shivered at how close he was. "Are you cold?" he asked.

Sarah shook her head, but Michael had heard and he stopped teasing Anne and asked, "You okay, Sarah?" She was very embarrassed. The last thing she wanted was for Jeff to know there was something wrong with her. She glared at Michael and shook her head again.

Someone tapped at the window and Michael's attention was diverted. "Elizabeth! What's she doing here?" He jumped up and hurried out to grab his sister. When he returned, Elizabeth was with him and it was obvious to everyone that Michael was upset. "Elizabeth, you sit here with Anne. I'll be right back."

"What's up?" Anne asked.

"He's just being mean and trying to get me in trouble. He's going to call Dad because I snuck out. He thinks Dad will be worried." Elizabeth took a long draft from Michael's drink and winkled her nose. "What is this?"

"It's a lime phosphate," Sarah said, "and what do you mean 'snuck out'? How did you get downtown?"

"Dad was busy, and I told him I was going over to Carol's, but instead I rode my bike down here and went to the movie. It was really good wasn't it? I think Jimmy Stewart is so handsome."

"Elizabeth." Michael reappeared, his voice tight with anger. "Dad is going to kill you. Where's your bike? I'm taking you home right now."

"I can ride my bike home. It's not even dark out yet."

"No, you can't! Come on! Sorry, everyone." He pulled Elizabeth out of the booth and then held out his hand to Anne. "I need to take my sister home right now."

Elizabeth was furious that Michael had "ratted her out" to her dad. She refused to speak to him and moped around the house, angry that she was restricted during her last days of summer. When the ban on visitors was lifted, Carol came over and she was able to vent. "It's so unfair. I just wanted to go to the movie. It wasn't like I was sneaking out to meet a boy or something. If I hadn't wanted to interrupt Michael's date, no one would have even known I was downtown. My dad makes the dumbest rules." Carol nodded. "If my mother lived here, I bet she'd understand."

"Did you talk to her?"

"I sent a letter. If I call, my dad will know because it's long distance."

"But why would he care if you call your mother. It doesn't cost that much to call Paris does it?"

"It's not about the money. They don't like each other." *And*, she added to herself, *they don't like me.*

"Parents are weird." Carol changed the subject. "Is Jeff still staying with Michael?" Elizabeth shook her head. "He's really cute. I wish I was old enough to date."

"Some girls at school date already."

"Yeah, but not us. Three more years! It's ridiculous."

"Sarah went out with Jeff, and she's only fifteen."

"When does Michael leave for college?"

"Next week, but I don't care." Elizabeth pushed her hair behind her ears and stared into the mirror. "I bet I could pass for sixteen if I cut my hair. And if I didn't have to wear that stupid uniform."

Michael left for college with only a perfunctory hug from Elizabeth. He knew she'd get over it, but his feelings were hurt. He still felt like she was his, and he hated to make her unhappy. He'd be home for Thanksgiving, but that was months away, and he knew he'd miss his kid sister.

Sarah was entering school - for the first time - as a senior and she was very excited. Her homeschooling had kept her current academically, but she knew that socially it might be difficult. She was still too weak to participate in sports, and she worried that she'd have no friends. Helen encouraged her to talk to Beth and to Elizabeth. "I know Elizabeth is younger than you, but she's been going to St. Agatha's since first grade."

As it turned out, Elizabeth was delighted to share her knowledge of the school, the cliques, the teachers, and which clubs were the best to join. Sarah listened avidly and grew more excited each day. Helen watched her cheeks flush and her breathing grow labored and worried that school would be too much for her to endure.

The City Chronicle
Thanksgiving, 1954

Tattletales by Sharon Chatsworth

Breaking with tradition, this year the Augustus family will not join together for Thanksgiving. Samuel Augustus and his family are instead in Arizona mourning the death of his father, Peter Augustus. Mary Elizabeth Augustus, sister to Peter, will be staying on in Arizona, and we will miss her gracious presence at events this holiday season. And, to the surprise of no one, certainly not to this reporter, Sylvia Augustus, wife of John, who is living on the continent, will remain on the continent.

Chapter Eighteen

John had flown out to Phoenix for his Uncle Peter's funeral, but he'd stayed only briefly. He was very concerned about Elizabeth and her attitude. It seemed like she was always angry and usually angry with him. He didn't understand it. He was hoping that Michael would be able to find out what was going on when he was home for the long Thanksgiving weekend. He took it as a good sign that Elizabeth had agreed to accompany him to meet Michael's train. And an even better sign when she almost jumped into Michael's arms as he stepped off the train. Maybe she'd just been feeling lonely.

On Friday, Michael suggested that he and Elizabeth take a long walk to look at the Christmas windows that the big stores were revealing that day, and, as a bonus, they'd be able to walk off yesterday's big meal. They bundled up against the cold and set out together, chatting a mile a minute. John smiled to see his darling Elizabeth happy again.

Elizabeth needed no encouragement to talk; Michael was her big brother and he'd always been there for her. She trusted him, and as soon as they were away from the house she asked, "I need to know about my mother, Michael."

"Know what?"

"Everything. Everything you know."

"I only know what you know. Valerie Smithson was a writer for a fashion magazine. She was a friend of Dad and Mother, and when she was killed in the Blitz they adopted you."

Elizabeth stopped walking and grabbed his arm. "Michael! That doesn't make sense. Mother never liked me, and you know that almost as soon as I was adopted she moved to Charleston, and she never talked to me again after that."

"I think that has more to do with their marriage than with you. Mother never liked me either and I don't think she liked being married."

"Didn't you ever ask?"

Michael started walking again and Elizabeth hurried to catch up. "Yes, of course, I asked. Dad said she loved me in the best way she could and that her moving away had more to do with money than anything else."

"What does that mean?"

"That they don't want to get a divorce, but they don't want to live together and that it is best for us to live with Dad because Mother drinks—drinks a lot."

"But…"

"But nothing, Elizabeth. We can't change anything, and we are lucky that Dad wants us."

"I really want to know about my real mother. I know she's dead, but she must have been married to someone and maybe he's still alive, and then I'd at least have one real parent."

"Have you talked to Dad about this? He was in England when you were born. He might have known your father."

"All he ever says is that Valerie was married to an Englishman who had disappeared before he ran into her in London, and that she died too soon after that for him to have asked all these questions. And then your nanny took us to safety, and he joined the RAF and that I know the rest of the story, and I don't! I love Dad but I want to know who I am! Everybody at my school has a family that goes back to the *Mayflower* and I have nobody."

"That's not true."

"Well, maybe not the *Mayflower*, but they have grandparents and great grandparents and names that match, and I'm adopted and I have nobody."

"You have me."

"Michael." Elizabeth was exasperated. "Some ghost gave me to you when I was born! You have me, I don't have you."

Her logic confused him, but he could see her point. "Isn't anyone else at your school adopted?"

"I don't think so. Do you know of anyone?" Michael shook his head, he couldn't think of anyone that was adopted, but guys didn't really talk about that stuff.

"And I'm darn sure no one else has a ghost mother."

"I haven't seen Valerie in a long time," Michael protested.

"Well, just in case, I sure haven't told anyone at school that story about my ghost mother giving me to you. Can you imagine what Barbara Hillis could do with that story?"

"If she's Jerry's sister, I can guess she's a bully and I can understand your concern. So don't mention that part of the story."

"I'm tired of being teased because I'm a war orphan whose adoptive mother hates her so much she has to go live in Paris."

Michael threw his arm over her shoulders and pulled her close in a swift hug. "I'll see what I can find out, okay? Just hang in there. High school will be over soon."

"Four more years! That's forever."

Before leaving on Sunday night, Michael found time to tell his dad about Elizabeth's questions. "I think you need to help her find out who her birth father was, Dad."

Inwardly, John blanched, but he managed to keep his face impassive. "I don't think I can do that. But maybe I can tell her more about her mother."

"That would help, I guess. But can't you find the marriage records for her mother and father? Then you could find out where he was killed and give her some facts."

"It's been thirteen years, Michael. Many of the records in England were destroyed in the Blitz, but I'll see what I can do."

John hated to lie; however, he had no intention of admitting that he was her birth father. Sylvia might be living in Paris, but he could just imagine the hell that letting the world know the truth would cause the entire family. Instead, he resolved to spend more time with Elizabeth and to see that she had everything she wanted. Perhaps next summer they could all go to Italy; she'd like that.

"There's one other thing, Dad." John raised his eyebrows questioningly. "I know this isn't a good time to talk about it, but I don't know what to do." John waited. "I saw Valerie last night."

"Michael," John started but then instead of rebuking him, he asked quietly, "Did she say anything?"

"She seemed very sad, and I thought she wanted to give me a message for Elizabeth, but instead she said that she would be waiting for Sarah and that she would take care of her."

Michael rubbed at his eyes, trying not to cry. "I think she meant that Sarah is going to die soon." He took a deep breath. "Do you think I should tell Aunt Helen? Or Christopher?"

John considered his answer carefully. "No," he said slowly. "I don't think you should tell anyone. I know it's hard, but Sarah is going to school. She's happy and busy. I know Helen and Sam are aware that her health is still precarious, and I don't think that knowing that you've spoken to Valerie would make things easier for anyone in the family. I think you need to keep this one to yourself. Perhaps it was just a dream, or perhaps she meant something else entirely."

John kept his word and spent more time with Elizabeth. She asked for pictures of her mother but John had none. He was able to tell her that Valerie had been orphaned shortly after the war broke out. He did find a few blurry newspaper shots that included Valerie in the background. She hadn't been a flashy dresser or one to want the spotlight. He gave her a copy of the obituary that her magazine had run after her death, and when she asked he had a copy of the headshot photo they had used blown up and framed. Elizabeth examined the photo carefully. "Do you think I look like her?"

"You look very much like her," John assured her. "She was smaller than you are going to be when you finish growing, and your hair is not quite as dark, but your eyes are the same beautiful brown, your mouth is exactly the same shape." His gut twisted as a vivid image of Valerie flashed before him. He managed to push it aside. "I know she would have been very proud to be your mother."

Elizabeth placed the photo on her bedside table and seemed to accept that John was unable to track down any information on her birth father.

In the summer of 1955, the family trip to Italy was a huge success and when Elizabeth saw the devastation that the bombing during the war had caused she told John she understood why he couldn't find her birth father's records. Elizabeth entered high school in the fall. She never mentioned Sylvia, so neither did he. But one night, he heard her telling her best friend, Jenny, that she had seen her mother in Italy, and he had to admit that perhaps she wasn't forgetting at all.

Certainly, they had not seen Sylvia in Italy, or anywhere else, but it seemed like a minor lie if it made her happy and better able to fit in at school, so he ignored that, too. Elizabeth was one of the youngest freshmen, but she quickly found a place on the school paper and often returned home late. Her grades were excellent and teachers praised her abilities. John continued to buy her anything she asked for and felt that they had dodged the "who's my real father?" bullet.

The City Chronicle
December 31, 1957

Tattletales by Sharon Chatsworth

For more than thirty years, this reporter has attempted to inform you and to entertain you, but our rapidly changing world is rather too much for me. The Beat Generation is changing attitudes and behaviors in ways that I do not understand. Only yesterday afternoon I saw with my own eyes Elizabeth Augustus (daughter of John and Sylvia Augustus) dressed all in black and skulking about with a group of young people.

But I digress; today's column is the last column I will write for this fine paper. Beginning Monday, my space will be filled with an advice column, *Dear Abby*, written by Abigail Van Buren. So farewell, my faithful readers, I will miss you.

Chapter Nineteen

Sylvia opened her copy of the *Chronicle* and quickly flipped to the Chatsworth column. Even now, after living in France for years, and receiving the paper late, she always read Chatsworth's column first. She was seldom mentioned these days, but the family was often commented on and today was no exception. It looked like John's bastard child might be causing problems. She certainly hoped so. Quickly, she read Chatsworth's farewell and grinned. *Good riddance to that bitch.* Sylvia toasted the paper with her glass of wine and poured another.

Perhaps I could live in the States again, she mused, but then she remembered the legal action against her. Sam had explained that as long as she stayed out of South Carolina, they would not press charges, and since there was nowhere else in the States she wanted to live, Paris was a perfect compromise. Her old friends still came over for visits, not as often as they had but people seemed busier now. And she'd made a great group of new friends here, expatriates, writers, artists, actors. There was somewhere to go and something to see every night. None of her new friends ever questioned why she was living in Paris without a husband or family. They simply accepted her as she was and loved her. She patted her hair into place and sipped at her wine.

Michael still sent an occasional note, but she never heard from that girl anymore, thank goodness, and John only communicated through the attorney. Patterson had finally died and she admitted to herself that that was a relief. He'd seemed so judgmental about every request for money she had made. John, on the other hand, had been very fair about the money, and he'd told the new attorney to give her anything she wanted, whenever she wanted it. Life here was good. She poured a bit more wine in her glass and headed for the bedroom to dress for dinner with the newest man in her life.

By unspoken agreement, the Augustus cousins and their dates were all gathered at Sam and Helen's for New Year's Eve. Everyone knew that Sarah's health was failing, and they wanted to be together. The fourteen young adults—Christopher, home on leave with a beautiful girl from California on his arm; Peter and his new wife, Evelyn; Jennifer and Geoff; Beth and her date, Bob, a tall guy with a strong Brooklyn accent; Michael and Anne; Elizabeth and a young man wearing a black turtleneck who she introduced simply as Lars; and Sarah and Jeff—had a great deal to discuss. Chatter and laughter filled the house as everyone brought everyone else up to date. Piles of records were stacked on the turntable and they all danced to the music of Guy Mitchell, Tab

Hunter, Perry Como, Andy Williams, and Pat Boone, but when Elvis Presley's "All Shook Up" and Buddy Knox's "Party Doll" came on, the parents watched and clapped from the sidelines. Helen kept a careful eye on Sarah to be sure she didn't overdo. She was pleased to note that Jeff managed to slow things down for Sarah without making it obvious. They made such a nice couple, she thought. Certainly, they were too young to be so serious, but Jeff had been Sarah's first boyfriend and as it turned out her only boyfriend.

As midnight approached, Sam filled glasses with champagne for everyone, and added flutes filled with 7 Up for those under twenty-one.

"Surely, Uncle Sam," Elizabeth said flirtatiously, "we are all old enough for a glass of champagne on New Year's Eve."

"Rules are rules, my dear," Sam said gallantly. "I'm an attorney you know."

Elizabeth wrinkled her nose and spoke quietly to her date. "What he doesn't know won't hurt him, I guess." Lars looked about and, seeing no one paying attention to them, added a generous splash from his pocket flask to each of their glasses. They grinned at each other and clinked once before joining the rest of the group for a toast.

The clock chimed and each member of the Augustus family saluted themselves and their dates and assumed that 1958 would be another banner year for the family.

And it was in many ways. In June, Beth, who had fulfilled her dream of working for a major magazine, received a doctorate from Radcliffe and accepted a teaching position at Columbia. Now her dreams involved women's rights first and fashion second. Sarah graduated from high school. Michael and Jeff graduated from college and accepted positions with AmCo. Elizabeth thought Michael was crazy to stay in the city and work for the family company, but Michael had seen Elizabeth in her black clothes and heard her spouting opinions on the importance of bettering one's inner self over and above material possessions and he worried about where she was heading and who her friends might be. He wanted to stay close to home.

In September, Elizabeth returned for her senior year at St. Agatha's. She allowed her hair to grow out long and wore it perfectly straight. At school, she pulled her hair back in the required ponytail and wore the school uniform, but when not in school she wore only black leotards and oversized black sweaters. John tried to entice her with shopping trips and offers of special nights out, but she withdrew and spent hours reading Jack Kerouac and John Clellon Holmes. She disappeared for long hours every weekend, and John had no idea who her friends were or what she was doing. Michael tried to draw her out, but she simply looked at him calmly and repeated that she was fine.

Sarah had chosen not to go to college. She and Jeff announced their engagement in December and started to plan a spring wedding. No one was surprised that they wanted to marry. Sarah seemed so much older than other girls her age, and she and Jeff obviously loved each other. Michael watched her flit about at her engagement party, and he remembered the last time he'd seen Valerie and thought she had been warning him about Sarah's death. Happily, he'd been wrong. Michael picked up his glass to propose a toast and there Valerie was, as solid as any other person in the room, right in front of him, blocking his view of the couple. She gazed at him sadly and shook her head. "She'll never marry, Michael." His hand shook violently, and he set his glass down and left the room. Glancing back at Sarah before leaving the room, he saw that she was watching him and he tried to smile.

Minutes later, Sarah joined him on the verandah. She laid her small hand on his arm. "I saw her, Michael. That was Valerie wasn't it?" In all these years, no one but Michael himself had ever mentioned seeing Valerie, but he knew that Sarah was telling the truth. He nodded. "I don't want you to tell me what she said. I know that I'm not going to live very long." He wanted to protest, but she continued, "It's all right, but it will be awful for Jeff and for my mother. You have to promise me that no matter what, you'll help them, help them go on."

Michael felt her calm certainty; he pulled her close in a hug and kissed her forehead. Someone tapped him on the shoulder. "Hey, that's my girl you're kissing," Jeff said.

"You forget, she's my favorite cousin and without me you two never would have met." Sarah tightened her arms around him in another quick hug. He understood what she needed and he smiled at her, let her go, and draped an arm over Jeff's shoulder. "Let's get back to the party. I want to make a toast to the happy couple."

Over the Christmas break, John took Elizabeth skiing in Colorado at the newly opened Aspen Highlands, but even the novelty of the manmade snow at Magic Mountain and the luxury hotel room didn't seem to interest her. Instead of joining with others from the city who were vacationing at the resort, Elizabeth wandered away and returned late each night smelling of smoke and what John was afraid might be marijuana.

When they returned from their vacation, it was only to learn that Sarah was in the hospital and not expected to live. Her fragile heart was finally stopping and this time there was no hope of another miracle operation. Elizabeth was furious at the news, raging about how unfair life was and that if there was a God, he'd never let someone like Sarah suffer. John and Michael tried to explain what a miracle her short life had been and what a blessing it was to have had her in the family and to have loved her even though it was truly too short a time. But Elizabeth was beyond listening to reason. She raged at John for not helping her find her real father and at Sylvia for adopting her and then leaving her and even at Michael, declaring to them all that they didn't love her.

Sam and Helen had always been the ones John turned to for parenting advice but now their grief consumed them. Finally, he called Sylvia, thinking that perhaps Elizabeth could go to Paris after graduation. But when Sylvia answered the phone, it was obvious that she was very drunk and John ended the call without suggesting that she invite Elizabeth for a visit.

After the funeral, Elizabeth was home less and less. She was cutting school and hanging out in coffee houses. Finally, after a particularly angry confrontation, she was able to elicit a promise from her dad that if she would do enough work to graduate, he would allow her to move to San Francisco and enroll in a college out there. With relief, John agreed. Surely a child he loved so much would have to come to understand that he loved her. Perhaps, as she kept insisting, she really did just need some space.

Chapter Twenty

Summer 1959

When John received the call from Sylvia's attorney telling him that she had died of what appeared to be a drug overdose, it shouldn't have come as a surprise, but it did. For a long minute, he said nothing, thinking of the beautiful girl he'd married. He heard the attorney's voice questioning, "Sir? Are you there?" He shook himself and managed to respond.

There were few details. She'd been found in bed by her housekeeper. The local police had confirmed her death, recording it as an "alcohol-induced drug overdose," with no evidence of foul play. Now they simply wanted to know what the family wished to do with the body. John couldn't imagine that Sylvia would want to be cremated, and he was sure that she would want to be buried in Charleston, so he gave the attorney the authority to take care of the details and arrange for her body to be returned to the States. After hanging up, he called Michael to his office and told him of his mother's death.

The tears that formed in Michael's eyes surprised him and he dashed them away. "We need to tell Elizabeth together, Dad. She's not going to take this well."

Elizabeth sat silently as her dad told her that her mother was dead. "Did she kill herself?" she asked calmly.

"The police didn't indicate that it was suicide, and I don't think so. Your mother loved life, and I think it was an accident."

"She wasn't my mother, Dad. She didn't even like me. She didn't like any of us. You know that. This isn't my real family."

"Elizabeth! How can you say that? I love you, and Michael loves you. Your cousins love you. Your aunt and uncle love you. We are your family."

"No, you sort of love me, I understand that, but you don't really love me, not the way you all love Michael. He's a real Augustus."

All of the family lies crashed around John. She was so wrong. And yet he was unable to tell her the truth. She was more a "real" Augustus than Michael would ever be. John didn't even know who Michael's birth father might be because Sylvia had refused to discuss it, and he'd lied to Elizabeth over and over again. Even now, with Sylvia dead, he didn't see how he could tell the truth; it would only make it worse. Instead, he told his children the plans that he'd made with the attorney and then the details of the funeral.

"Do I have to go?" Elizabeth asked.

"Of course you do. You may not like it, but she was your mother."

Elizabeth started to protest again and changed her mind. "As soon as the funeral is over, I want to move to San Francisco. I've applied to San Francisco State College, and I think they'll accept me. I know classes don't start until September, but I have some friends who will let me stay with them until I can move into the dorm."

"Friends? What friends?"

"Just this girl from school. Her older sister goes to San Francisco State, and she said we could visit her this summer."

"Why am I only hearing about this now?" John asked.

"Well, I didn't think you'd let me go, but now I think you can see that I need to get away from here as soon as possible. I can't pretend that I miss a mother who never liked me."

John actually had to admit that what she was saying might make sense. San Francisco was clear across the nation, but... "I'll think about it," he said.

Elizabeth and Michael were calm throughout the burial. It had been a long time since John had seen them standing close, hands touching, and his heart lifted. Michael might not have been his birth son, but he had turned out to be everything he wanted in a son. Surely, Elizabeth would grow out of this rebellious stage. He knew that young people had always questioned their family's values, but the media articles about this Beat Generation were just making it worse. They were selling Elizabeth and her friends on a way of life that seemed like dangerous fun, a lifestyle that condemned everything that the Augustus family had always stood for: decency, honor, social responsibility, and, of course, capitalism.

With the number of classes Elizabeth had managed to skip in her senior year, John confessed to Sam that he was very happy she had managed to be admitted to San Francisco State College. He worried that she would be so far from home but knew that it was what she wanted. And, after meeting Sherry's family and being assured that her older sister was indeed willing to have Elizabeth stay with her for a few days and then settle her into her room in Merced Hall, John allowed Elizabeth to pack her clothing and put her on a plane to San Francisco. She promised to call home at least once a week and hugged both Michael and John before boarding.

Elizabeth called on arrival as she had promised. She called again a few days later, very excited about everything she had seen and done. Her third call came after moving into the residence hall and meeting her new roommate. Then the calls stopped. John imagined that she was busy making friends and attending classes. He tried not to worry, but after three weeks of calling the residence hall and being told she wasn't available, he was truly frightened, and he called and asked for the housemother.

"Elizabeth Augustus?" Fear shot through John as he heard the question in the woman's voice. "Mr. Augustus, your daughter moved out of the residence hall last week."

"Why? Where did she go?"

"She provided a letter from you giving your permission, so there was no need for us to contact you. I'm sure she will have changed her address at the registration office. Do you need that number?" John assured her that he had the number. "I'll check with the girls and if I learn anything more, I'll call you at once. If you have further questions, you may call me at any time."

Shocked and fearful, John managed to say thank you and hang up the phone.

With the death of his father, Sam had assumed the role as patriarch of the Augustus family. He'd refused to move into the office that Walter had once occupied. Instead, after Peter's death they'd turned that big corner office into the boardroom, and he and John often met there to hammer out company business. Returning from lunch, his secretary took his coat and informed him that John and Michael were waiting for him in Walter's office. He smiled to hear the room called that. It was often funny how long it took for old habits to die. Walter had been dead almost fifteen years now but perhaps his ghost was still roaming the building. He was grinning at the thought as he pushed open the door. One look at John's face and the smile faded. "What's up, Cuz?"

Sam removed his glasses and polished the lenses as he listened. John finished with, "You look just like Grandfather when you do that. He always said it helped him think, and I hope it'll help you because I don't know what to do."

"Obviously, we need to find her. If she's dropped out of school, she could be anywhere." The stress in Michael's voice reflected the fear John felt.

"The registrars' office said she hasn't been in class this week, but that doesn't necessarily mean she's dropped out of school. Maybe she's sick or hurt. If she was dropping out, certainly, she'd go to the office and let them know."

"Dad, do you really think she has any respect for authority? All she's talked about for over a year is 'dropping out and dropping in.' How she wants to open up her inner self and live authentically without material possessions."

"I don't even know what that means. She's eighteen. She's not old enough to live on her own."

"Well," Sam spoke, "legally she is. But I think the first item of business is to find her."

"I'll go as soon as I can get a flight." John jumped to his feet.

"Not the best idea, Cuz. I think we need to hire someone to talk to her friends and then send Michael to talk some sense into her. And..." He hesitated. "...it might be time to tell her the truth."

John stilled. Michael watched the two men he admired most in the world as they struggled with the idea of releasing family secrets.

Finally, John spoke, looking directly at Michael. "Elizabeth is my daughter. Valerie and I wanted to get married but it seemed impossible for us to get a divorce and then... she was killed."

"I think I knew that," Michael said. "I'm not sure why, but I think I knew. There had to be a reason why Mother hated her so much. Do you think if we find her and tell her the truth that it will make her happy?"

"I have no idea," Sam replied. "It may make it worse, but at least if she has the truth she will be dealing with facts instead of looking for a fictional father."

"And I'm not her brother, either, am I?" Michael looked toward John. "If my mother isn't her mother and you're not my father, I'm not her brother. You've been a great father since Mother moved to Paris, but who is my father? Do you know?"

"I don't, Michael. Sylvia never told me. But I consider you my son in every way. I admit that I didn't always feel that way, but now I do. I'm proud to call you my son, and I certainly consider you Elizabeth's brother."

"But Elizabeth won't. If you think knowing you've been her 'real' father all along will make things right, I'm afraid you don't understand how angry she is. A life built on lies is exactly what she has been protesting against, and now she's going to be told that she is right and that you have been lying all along."

John stared out the window, shaking his head slowly. "What can I do? How can I fix this?"

Sam thought about all the family secrets and lies that he knew; many that John didn't know himself. Was it time to tell all or would that destroy the family and the AmCo dynasty? As time passed, the lies had become reality and now the old lies had been buried and forgotten. Somehow, Michael had figured out his parenthood, and it seemed fair that Elizabeth should learn the truth about hers. Perhaps this younger generation could begin to live without lies and secrets. "First, we need to find Elizabeth, and then we need to tell her and everyone else in the family the truth about our family history. It's time for the Augustus family to come clean, at least with each other. We'll make this work."

Elizabeth has disappeared into the subculture of the early hippy movement. What began for her in the city as she lingered in coffeehouses with the beatniks is transforming her. Her desire to know who she really is has led her to drop out of college and move away - away - to where no one in the Augustus family will ever find her.

Watch for *Family Myths*, Book 3 of the
Augustus Family Trilogy
Publication in the fall of 2015.

Thank you for reading *Family Matters*

You can contact me on my Amazon Author
Page
Or
My blog **Book A Day Habit**
Or
Email me at **tamara@tamaramerrill.com**

A Note About The Author

Tamara Merrill, is an MBA turned writer or perhaps that should be a writer turned MBA turned fiction writer. She began writing as a child, submitting multiple stories to *American Girl* magazine that were never published. But in the sixties and seventies her short stories were published in the woman's magazines of the day and now she is writing novels. She is available for book signings and appearances as book club meetings, either through Skype or in person. She writes a blog titled BOOK A DAY HABIT where she chronicles her reading and writing adventures. You can email her at tamara@tamaramerrill.com.

www.ingramcontent.com/pod-product-compliance
Lightning Source LLC
Chambersburg PA
CBHW070842250626
47159CB00003B/891